I0519690

SHOUT

Noelle Bodhaine

Copyright © 2015 Noelle Bodhaine

Published by Naughty Nellies Pervy Press

All rights reserved.

ISBN: 0692553010
ISBN-13: 978-0692553015

Colleen
Irish meaning Girl
Colleen
Editor
Therapist
Wife
Mother
Nurse
Realist
Goddess
Collaborator
Mentor
Voice of Reason
Shoulder
Friend
Thank you for all you've done
Your time, energy, humor and encouragement
have been invaluable.
To express my gratitude would take chapters.
Without you Rhys would be trapped and Sophie would
never have grown. I wouldn't have grown.
Thank you for believing in me.

ACKNOWLEDGMENTS

Thank You
Merci, Grazie, Go Raibh Maith Agaibh,
Simple words of gratitude
that will never be enough.
It has taken a team
to get Rhys and Sophie to the stage.
I am profoundly in debt to everyone who has
helped me, near and far.
To those who are aware of their impact
and those who are not,
You are indelibly written into the fabric
of Rhys and Sophie's story and now my own.
The passion and ambition
of the independent writer
is stoked by readers.
It is a partnership fed by fantasy and escape
I promise to keep fantasizing
if you promise to keep escaping with me!
Merci, Grazie, Go Raibh Maith Agaibh
Thank You
ENJOY!

Whisper it in my ear,
Speak the words out loud
Hell,
Shout it from the Goddamn
rooftops if you must
Just put
Voice to your desires
And I will fulfill every single one
-Rhys Slate

Ch. 0.5

I took his touch when I left. Ghostly whispers of his fingers skating across my heated skin woke me from a deep, unsettling sleep for the first few nights. Melissa also tagged along. Her deep brown eyes mocking me from behind my own lids, her face full of pleasure, her mouth full of rubber.

It took more than a week for the fog to lift. Rhys has that effect on me, a respite that I need to recover from, stripping me of good sense and a strong will. Yet, even as I open my eyes to the rising autumn sun, my mind is shrouded in thoughts of him, his fingers brushing the hair from my face, his lips soft and wet on the curve of my back, his strong hands holding my hips as he plunders my body. I miss him. I reach for my vibrating phone and another sign that I made the wrong choice.

Good Morning, Beautiful. I don't know about you, but I have not been sleeping well, my bed feels so empty without you, my house so cold. Although I have tried to do as you wish, I find my desire for you cannot be denied. You are the one thing in this life that has allowed me the possibility of being something different, someone different. I would be a fool to let you go, it would be to abandon the very possibility of my better self.

A variation of the same message, every

morning since I left. I thought being away from him would afford me a little clarity, that I would discover in the bright light of a Rhys free day that I didn't really need him, that it was all contrived, not real. But it is real. It is so real I can taste his skin on my tongue. I hear his voice in my dreams. This is real and suddenly I want to drop everything and run. Run back to New York, back into his arms and apologize. Apologize for leaving, for ever thinking that I could fight this, for ever denying that I needed him.

I sit up and call him immediately.

"Good Morning, Beautiful." His warm voice slides through the phone and he comes rushing back into my bloodstream. Like a shot of adrenaline, my heart beats stronger and I am alive again. I didn't realize how much I missed him, missed that voice. I need to hear him, for him to call me Beautiful every day. I want to go back.

"Good morning," the softest whisper before my voice cracks.

"I miss you, Sophie."

"I miss you, too."

"I want you to come back, and stay, in New York. Please, come back." Tears swell in my eyes and I take a deep, cleansing breath. The deepest breath I have taken in ages and all at once I am full and so empty.

"Rhys."

"Sophie," he cuts me off, "I love you." My heart stops and my life in *loves* flashes quickly behind my eyes. I am acutely aware that no *love* has ever felt like that, like the all-consuming comfort of a warm flame that you know won't harm you, the slow sweet flow of honey that coats your throat. His love is all I have ever needed. He just filled me up, just like that, three little words that I have heard a million times, but never really felt, until now. My tongue is limp in my mouth, my mind raging so loudly that I cannot hear a thing. This man loves me! This man loves me, me. Sophie.

I don't know how long the silence lasts as I contemplate the prize I have just been given. My mind races to catch up and the last few months' flash before me. How much has changed. How full and open my heart feels, like a rolling meadow with no end in sight my feelings for him know no horizon. No ending, I will surely swell and burst.

"I love you, too!" I cannot get the words out fast enough, I am bursting.

"Jesus, Beautiful, that felt amazing. Say it again."

"I love you." I reply with a smile that I know he can hear, as I can hear his. The tilt of his grin, the crinkle in his eyes, I can feel it in my heart. I fucking love this man. And he loves me.

"Come back." A quiet, but forceful demand that I will gladly fulfill.

"I want to. I will."

"Today."

"Rhys, I have some things that have to be taken care of. Today, I have a meeting at the bank, liquidating everything I own to try and save my grandmother's house. I have to finish packing up all her stuff. I am almost done, I promise."

"I don't want to wait, Sophie. I fucking need you in my arms right now." The urgency is palpable in his voice, his tone colored now with anxiety and impatience.

"Tomorrow. I think I can be done with everything and be ready to go by tomorrow."

"Let's shoot for tonight," he quickly replies. I hear a muffled voice in the background and the distinct sound of a hand covering the phone, before he returns. "Sophie, my love." The words settle heavily between us, pulling us together. "I have a few meetings this morning and lunch with my father and then I will call you. Do you think you will be at the bank by then?"

"My appointment is at noon."

"Okay, Beautiful, I want you to call me as soon as you finish at the bank, and we will make all the arrangements. I cannot stand the idea of another night away from you. I need you, Sophie. I need you now." If it was possible to overdose on happiness I would surely be a writhing pile of limbs on the floor right now. My heart feels so full that it could burst in my chest and my lips are on the verge of cracking from the force of a smile the likes I have never experienced. I am done. This is it.

"Yes, Rhys, I will call you."

"I can't wait, Sophie. I cannot wait to tell you I love you in person. I need to see your face, Beautiful. It's killing me not to see you. You have made me so happy. I have to run, until later, my love."

"I love you," I reply before he is abruptly gone, and I am left to my pounding heart and love fogged mind.

The morning slips away in a jumble of busy work and day dreaming. Floating away and wasting time with Rhys, locked in a room until neither of us can take another moment. Working as hard as I can with such a consuming distraction on my mind. After I sign my life away at the bank, I treat myself to lunch from the dollar menu. Such is my life now. And I head to my grandmother's house to pack the last few boxes. I wait to call Rhys, giving myself an hour. An hour to get as much done as possible, knowing as soon as we speak, the wheels will be in motion. When I finally come up for air, I find my phone rattling away on the kitchen counter. Twenty-five missed calls. And it jumps to life in my hand.

"Sophie! Where have you been? I have been trying to reach you forever!"

"I have been at the bank, signing away every

penny I have or ever will have, to try and save Lola's house. And now I am packing. Why? What is going on?"

"Rhys…" She hangs his name out, breathes, and leaves it hanging. "He was in an accident, Sophie. He and Michael."

"What?" The breath rushes from my chest, replaced by a tangible, strangling panic. A panic so virile I can taste it. I have been here before.

"He and Michael were in a car accident. You should get here, Sophie. It's serious." The panic in her voice pushes me over the precipice. My heart drops to the floor. A dead thud fills my head. My knees give way and I sink to the cold, hard tile.

"Sophie, are you still there?" The phone suddenly feels like dead weight. Lead in my hand. I struggle to bring it back to my ear.

"I'm still here," I manage, choking on grief.

"You need to get here fast." I look down at my wrist, and the sparkling, over the top gift. The icy cold, heavy watch that Rhys insisted upon buying. *The gift of time,* he quipped. The only thing I own of any worth. The only thing I own now, of any value, real personal value. I have to get to him.

***

The flight, the cab ride, everything is a blur. I am numb and exhausted. The only thing I feel is the urgent pull to get to the hospital, to get to him. I need to tell him I am sorry. I need to tell him the truth.

The hum and chaos of the city can't even touch me. I see New York through the window, passing by, teeming with life. Cars weave and bob past us, horns blaring but I hear none of it. Throngs of people flow up and down packed sidewalks, crossing traffic in waves, I don't see a single face. All I can see is my past flashing before my eyes, the searing, white hot pain and anticipation of losing everything.

We pull up to Mt. Sinai and I am frozen. Stuck in the sticky, worn, back seat, my eyes scale the ominous black tower rising from the center of the hospital. The cab driver bangs on the partition, demanding his fare and my exit. I pull what cash I have left from my hastily packed purse and push a twenty through the slot. He laughs, a deep chortle, before he begins to yell in a language I do not understand. Banging his chubby fist on the partition, he stabs his short dirty fingers at the meter. He is animated and exasperated, the meter reads $64.20. God damn, this city is going be the death of me, and my meager pockets.

The city is stagnant. Humidity hangs in the September air like a shroud. Coating everything in an exhaust filled, grimy mist. Never have I been so assaulted by my surroundings. Turning my eyes to the dark night sky, caught in the looming shadow of the sleek, black tower, I imagine Rhys, lying in that prophetic building. Please, don't let me be too late! I hear my name, carried on a hot breeze, and it feels like a bad dream. I turn towards the entrance when Olivia appears, as if out of thin air.

"Sophie! You're here, thank God." Dazed and caught off guard, I grab her arm to steady me.

"Um....yeah. I am here." She holds me at arm's length, headlights flash across her eyes and she shakes her head.

"Sophie, I know Rhys would want you here, but you cannot go in there now."

"What? Why?" Inside, I am pushing past her, rushing to Rhys' side. I look down to find my feet anchored to the dirty sidewalk, as Olivia stands before me with an all too familiar grief in her eyes.

"Listen to me. He is in really bad shape. They have him in an induced coma. But his mother and Nadja are up there. I cannot let you go in there. They are chomping at the bit, and they will eat you alive. Rhys would not want that, and neither do I."

"But…What? Why is she here? What am I supposed to do?"

"Matthew is in there with them. He will keep us posted, and let us know as soon as they leave. There is nothing we can do for him now anyhow."

"Olivia." My voice cracks as I wipe away the first heavy tear, I held it at bay as long as I could. "What if it's too late?"

"It won't be. They are doing everything they can. He is in very capable hands." She pulls me toward a waiting Town Car, the driver casually leaning on the hood watching our exchange. He scrambles to open the back door as Olivia gives him a signal. "Come, let's get you settled, and we will wait for word from Matthew."

"Settled?" I yank my hands from hers, angry, frustrated and quickly sinking into an abyss. It's all too much, our petty squabble, the accident, his mother, and Nadja. I came all the way here just to be turned away? I cannot stand the thought of him lying there alone. But the thought of Nadja being at his side stokes a distracting, if not comforting rage. "Where are we going?" I don't want to go anywhere. I want to plant myself at the hospital, at Rhys' side. His mother and Nadja be damned! The car pulls out, seamlessly blending into the heavy traffic. Olivia squeezes my hand, pulling my attention from the disappearing hospital.

"You will come and stay with me and Matthew." She holds her hand in the air, cutting off my inevitable protest. "Stop, I won't hear anything about it. I am doing this for you, and you are going to let me. I am just so sorry this is happening."

The remainder of the ride is silent. The sound of my pounding heart and my racing pulse drown out Olivia and the rest of the city.

CH. 1

Twelve days. Two hundred and eighty-eight hours, seventeen thousand two hundred and eighty minutes. Thirty-five hours of sleep, three bottles of scotch, and one wounded man.

The first two days are blurred, my world had never been quite so dark; my heart slowed, my mind wandered and got lost somewhere. Tangled in the depths of blue the likes of which I had never experienced, a formless mass of disbelief, denial and anger. Day three I had no choice but to pull myself up.

I knew that even in the shallow pits of my personal despair a bigger storm was brewing, and if I didn't monitor the situation it was bound to get out of hand. I packed a bag and headed to the Hamptons and into the clutches of the succubus. I wasn't going to allow Nadja to be alone with my mother. The weekend in the Hamptons was a bad idea, but I inserted myself in the middle. I should have known what to expect, I *did* know what to expect, and yet, I let my fucking guard down.

We had just finished a marathon poker tournament and I was several scotches down, my pockets were significantly lighter, and I was completely distracted. The long walk from the main house to the pool house did nothing to help me focus; I was getting fuzzier as the minutes passed. I didn't remember leaving the sliding glass doors open to the pool, but I could see the god-awful gauzy blue curtains blowing in the breeze. As I slipped inside, I quickly pulled my shirt over my head and tossed it over the back of the couch and made my way towards the bathroom and a cool shower.

Under the pounding water I closed my eyes and pictured Sophie; her soft skin, the curve of her hip, the twist of her smile, fuck, I missed her. I let my mind wander and I begged the water to wash clean my liquor soaked heart; her smile, her smell, her taste. Yet, with every memory of her came a nightmare that starred Nadja. When I closed my eyes, I saw her smug face and then Sophie's shocked horror.

I scrubbed my skin raw as anger stoked under the falling water, doing my best to wash myself clean of Nadja. exiting the shower, I fucking slammed the glass door and made it rattle and bow. I wiped the water away from my body, and examined myself in the mirror, but something was missing; forever missing, the warm caress of her hands around my belly, the soft press of her round breasts against my back.

All the reasons Sophie was not here came rushing into my mind, and when I stumbled out of the bathroom there she was, *the reason*. Nadja lay draped across my bed like a teenaged girl, legs kicked in the air and her chin rested in her palms.

She winked and cat called before I was aware of my nakedness and I quickly pulled on a pair of shorts. This was all because of *her*. I cannot help but tally every little thing Nadja has done to throw a wrench in my relationship with Sophie. Every underhanded move she ever made was all calculated and executed with precision.

"What are you doing here, Nadja?"

"Kylie wasn't feeling well and I'm bored. I thought we could have a drink."

"No, Nadja, I don't want to have a drink with you. I have had quite enough and would love nothing more than to put a cap on this day. Now, if you don't mind…" I extended my arm and wavered slightly as I pointed towards the door, but she just grinned and tucked her legs beneath her, digging her heels in, denying my not so subtle request. With a heavy sigh, I resigned myself and knew if I wanted to get rid of her, I first would have to give in. I walked to the kitchen to pour her a drink. When I turned around, she was right behind me, a shadow, she mirrored my every move, a darkness that followed me, unshakeable. I pushed a glass into her hand and waited, but she just stood there, watched me; her fake passive mask barely held in place.

"Won't you drink with me? I do hate to drink alone." I stood still and watched her eyes as they flared, as she struggled to maintain her syrupy sweet demeanor. "I believe Bianca would be appalled by your hospitality, Rhys."

"Then the feeling would be mutual. I am often appalled by *her* brand of hospitality, but if it will get you out of here sooner I'll have one drink. I'm going to grab a shirt." Wanting nothing more than to hide myself from her sickly possessive gaze, I stomped into my room and ripped a T-shirt from its hanger. I tugged it angrily over my head before I lost my foot and fell to the bed. God damn it, I was in no mood and in no state for her right then. White hot anger churned with the scotch and I was tired, tired of this damn dance, tired of being forced into corners by her behavior; one drink.

When I returned to the kitchen, she was seated at the table with two rocks glasses in front of her. As I took my seat, she pushed one of the glasses in my direction and grinned.

"Just a drink, Rhys, nothing more." Her sickly sweet smile turned my delicate stomach and I bit back a gag.

"You will forgive me if I don't take you at your word." I swirled the scotch around the glass and watched her take a deep drink.

"I'll always forgive you, Rhys, I often wonder, though, if you would afford me the same courtesy."

"And what, pray tell, do you have to forgive me for?"

"Come now, Rhys, you cannot believe yourself

completely blame free?"

I lifted the glass to my lips in an attempt to silence my surely forked tongue and she helped as she tipped the glass to my lips with her fingers.

"That's it, Rhys, drink up. I just want to talk." I let the scotch luge down my throat, the whole glass, one gulp, and she released her held breath. "Now that we have that over with, let's talk about Sophie, shall we?" And at the mere mention of her name, as the angelic sound passed through the gates of Hell, I lost my temper and everything became a blur.

"Don't you talk about her, Nadja, don't you dare." The cool malice in my voice took me by surprise and the air chilled between us. I pushed back from the table and stand with a sway while Nadja remained in her seat.

"She is a child, Rhys, a nobody's child, and she will never be good enough for you. I am sorry to say, but you are making a fool out of yourself." I grabbed her chair and pulled her out from the table. She stood and I placed my hand firmly on her back gently shoving her towards the sliding glass door and the open pool deck.

"You have to go," I growled as we approached the open door.

"Rhys, wait!" she yelled, feigning fear, as she tried to pull at my heartstrings, but she cut those strings a long time ago. I am so far past the end of my rope nothing she could say will pull me back.

She tried to push against me to stop me from pushing her, but I was determined. As we made it to the door, she pushed back against me with all her might and forced me to push back, and she lost her footing. I grabbed her by the arm to stop her from falling but she ripped herself from my hands, which sent her slight frame hurling towards the door jamb where she crumbled to the floor. I stopped and watched her like a slow motion movie. She looked up into my eyes with first a smile, a smile that chilled my blood and then she erupted into tears, her face cradled in her hands.

"Rhys, how could you?" She scurried to her feet while I stood cemented in place, unbelieving. "I can't believe this is who you've become. You are not the man I used to love." She turned and rushed out in dramatic fashion, which left me stunned, confused and even fuzzier than before she arrived. I barely made it back to the bedroom before everything faded to black.

When I awoke on Sunday, I had slept through brunch and a large chunk of my memory was missing. Kylie was noticeably upset, saying that Nadja left in the night with only a note of apology, explaining she had booked a last minute job. *Thank God for that.* After eighteen holes of golf and a light supper, it was time to go back to the city, back to reality. Monday could not come soon enough.

CH. 2

Monday morning, she rolls into my office like a dark cloud, large glasses covering her eyes and a loose sweater wrapped around her shoulders. She sits before my desk and slowly lowers her glasses, revealing the shadow of a black eye and I notice the remnants of a split lip. Her skin is sallow and dull and she looks like she hasn't slept in days, I push back from my desk stunned.

"What has happened to you?" Shock is evident in my tone, but her face is passive.

"You really don't remember?" Her pale lips twist in a cool smirk.

"Remember what? What are you talking about, Nadja?"

"Rhys, you did this," she pauses and touches her cheek for effect, "you did this to me."

"What the hell are you saying?"

"Saturday night you invited me back to the pool house and we had a drink. We were making up." The unbruised side of her mouth twists with an oddly sweet grin. "We made up a few times actually." As she says it, I am racking my brain while my stomach turns, combing through memories and Saturday is blank. I played poker, everything else is black; *this is not happening, this did not happen.* I calmly push my chair back from my desk and stand slowly, watching her every move. She flinches and sinks back in her chair as I walk around my desk, and I am thrown when she feigns fear. I think better of getting any closer and instead turn my back. *This cannot be happening.* I struggle and fight to recall Saturday night and can't. Poker, scotch, nothing, *fuck*! What the hell have I done? I turn back towards her and she is watching me with baited breath.

"I have absolutely no recollection of what you're accusing me of, Nadja."

"Are you calling me a liar, Rhys? Look at me, did I do this to myself?" She raises her voice for a short moment before quickly lowering her volume, but dialing up the menace. "You believe what you want to believe, Rhys, but the damage is done. All I need is to be photographed like this and people will start asking questions. Shall I direct them to you?"

"You wouldn't!" The words fall out in a desperate rush.

"I would," she says with a raised eyebrow, "I think we both know that. Now, I am tired of these games, Rhys. I am willing to take you back and to forget this ever happened."

"What the hell are you talking about?" I ask, as my world spins off its axis.

"I will protect your secret, Rhys. I will protect us," she says, standing up slowly, prowling towards me. She rests her hands on my shoulders and whispers into my ear, "I won't let anyone know what kind of man you really are. We can fix this together. I promise, baby, it will all be alright." I back away from her and see nothing but evil flickering in her eyes, her dull, blackened eyes. *I did that?*

"We will get through this together and we will be stronger for it, you'll see." She reaches up to cup my cheek and I catch her by the wrist, watching it in slow motion. My fist closes around her bony arm and she smiles with a gleeful umbrage that would frighten the devil. *Fuck, what have I done?*

The next few days are agony as she holds her bruises over me, reminding me every day of the jobs she had to cancel or risk *me* being discovered. Drowning in guilt and confusion and doubt, I think of Sophie, her sprinting across the grass that night, the fear in her eyes, the relief when our eyes met, the way she trembled in my arms. *How could I have done this?*

I get a sick relief when Nadja leaves town for a few days and I am finally rid of the sight of her. I could never be good enough for Sophie. Would she ever forgive me? There's no way, I am trapped.

The relief almost drowns me when I hear from Nadja that she will be taking a week of rest with her mother. Every morning I send Sophie a message, a lie. I cannot let her go. I cannot get her out of my head. I need to get her back. Every day, I fight a battle between the swell of my heart for the growing love I have for Sophie and the ever growing pit of despair and guilt I have, eating me alive, over what I've done to Nadja. I tap out my morning message to Sophie as I sit at my desk.

Good Morning, Beautiful. I don't know about you, but I have not been sleeping well, my bed feels so empty without you….

"Good morning, Mr. Slate." Nina enters my office with a nod and my espresso. Placing the cup on the corner of my desk, she goes about her morning routine, raising all the blinds, sorting my mail and looking over my shoulder as I plead for Sophie's return. When my phone rings, my heart leaps into my chest. Finally, I am able to say the words I have been dying to say.

"Good Morning, Beautiful." The faint sound of her breathing slides through the phone and she comes rushing back into my bloodstream. Like a shot of adrenaline, my heart beats stronger and I am alive again. I didn't realize how much I need her, what strength she brings. I want to tell her she is beautiful every day. I want her back.

"Good morning," her soft whisper breaks my heart.

"I miss you, Sophie."

"I miss you, too." *Oh, thank God!*

"I want you to come back and stay in New York. Please, come back." I take a deep, cleansing breath. The deepest breath I have taken in ages and all at once I am full and so empty, waiting with baited breath for her answer.

"Rhys."

"Sophie," I cut her off, unable to hold back another moment; "I love you."

I tell her I love her and that I want her back. *Now.* I didn't realize how heavy those words have been on my heart until I say them aloud, literally setting myself free. And then she says them back. I must have left my body for a moment, elated.

CH 3

I awaken on the first morning with a dark hatred weighing heavily on my fragile heart. I dreamt of Rhys, his warm lips, his strong hands. Yet every time I could muster a visual, it was of a broken and battered soul being lorded over by a succubus. *Nadja.* She lives in my subconscious and somehow I am her prisoner. Why is she suddenly posted up next to his bedside like some twisted Florence Nightingale? I don't understand why Matthew wants to keep me away so badly, he has insisted since the moment he came home and found me curled up on his couch that I was not to go to the hospital without him under any circumstance. I've never known Matthew to be a brute, but that is the only proper word to describe him. Since the moment I arrived, he has been on edge, brooding and bossy. Even Olivia seems to be put off, but she remains silent, tossing him snotty looks behind his back, rolling her eyes at me, yet not letting me out of her sight. Whatever the reason for his keeping me away, she is clearly on board.

The sweetest reprieve arrives in the form of Matthew's mother for tea and a grill session with Olivia. She is ready for grandchildren and is not shy about saying so, almost every day since the wedding apparently. I duck out under the guise of a run while Olivia is too battered and distracted to stop me. I run until my lungs burn and my eyes

water, almost three blocks. I hate running. I decide
to reward myself with a bagel and start walking,
searching for a bakery.

I find myself less than two blocks away from
the hospital and I cannot stop my feet. Just a quick
peek, what's the harm? Being away from him is
agony; every moment he lays there without me by
his side is a moment we have lost, never to get
back. I stand across the street for a tortured
moment, wanting so badly to bolt upstairs and
demand answers, demand to see his face and know
he is okay, to feel his heart beating, see his chest
rise and fall. I take a deep breath and muster my
bravery.

Visitors and nurses shuffle in and out of the
main doors. The place is bustling and I decide to
walk around the block and find another door. I dash
across the street when I think it's safe only to be
narrowly missed by an asshole in a yellow taxi who
lays on the horn and waves his arms sending my
pulse skyrocketing. Startled, shaken, and out of
breath, I slink around the corner, feeling slightly
anxious when I'm stopped dead in my tracks. My
ears twitch and burn from the seductive grating of a
Russian purr that I will never forget. I peek around
the corner of a dirty alleyway and see a couple, half
in the throes of passion, half at one another's
throats, whispered anger, hushed demands, and
grabby hands.

There is an edge in her voice, a fear, if I believe her to be capable of such an emotion. When I look again, I am shocked to see her raised against the wall like a pitiful rag doll, her feet dangling off the ground. The beast has her by the throat, nose to nose. I can't hear a word he says, but I know it's not good. She just gazes into his eyes, nodding, her face slowly turning pink, her eyes wide with shock, a single mammoth tear rolling down her face.

I back around the corner and take a deep breath, not wanting to get caught watching, but unable to walk away, even from Nadja. When I dare to take another look, she is back on her feet, rubbing her neck where his hand just was, as he presses his palm to her belly. Grasping her chin, he forcefully raises her lips to his and claims her mouth as his own in a wholly possessive, heated kiss that screams ownership.

She gasps for air when he lets her go pressing herself into the wall as he steps even closer, robbing any of her personal space that remained. With his hands on both sides of the wall, he leans in and I am frightened for her, until I see her hands snake around his waist and she pulls him closer. Her boney arms barely wrap around his massive form and she buries her face in his shoulder, weeping, seeking comfort from the very monster that caused her pain. It seems we have more in common than either of us would ever like to admit. Breaking the kiss, she turns in my direction and I quickly turn and dash for the street and the safety of a few blocks distance, upset that I let myself feel even a momentary concern for her.

I turn in the opposite direction and start the long walk back to Olivia and Matthew's, pondering that massive hand around her throat, the fear in her eyes and her quick relent. That was passion, dark and twisted, evident even from afar. I wander the morning streets after stopping for an expensive cup of coffee and a bagel that I have no intention of eating.

I don't tell Olivia what I did or that I even considered trying to see him without her or Matthew, not wanting her to alert Matthew and lose what little freedom of information I did have. I just sat on it and thought, plotted how to get to him, to get around Nadja. My mind reels at the possibilities, and the obvious reality that she is entwined with that brute. Rhys lays helpless at the mercy of his mother and this deceptive bitch. It makes me angry to the point of tears; heavy, angry, reflective tears for two solid days.

The third night post-accident, Olivia was able to coax me out of my plotting and growing self-pity temporarily with wine and nibbles. She came home with a wrapped bottle of Chianti and fried ravioli from the little Italian restaurant on the corner.

"I'm so sorry to hear about Lola's house,

Sophie. I know how much her house meant to you. Is there nothing you can do?" She sets the bottle down with three empty jelly jars, prompting Matthew to pour us each a glass.

"It's already done. Every cent I was able to scrape together barely covered her debts. I could never have come up with the money to actually buy the house." I take a slow drink from the dry wine and feel Lola pulsing through my body; her hot Italian blood, wise beyond measure, stubborn beyond reason. "It'll go up for auction soon."

She was the strongest woman I have ever known, always on her own, born to be a matriarch, her mother before her was the same way by outliving four, count them, four husbands, and raised her girls alone. My Lola did the same. She outlived my grandfather who lived just long enough to see my father smile. She raised her three children on her own, in a time when that was practically unheard of. My uncle, her pride and joy, didn't make it through Vietnam. When I think of all that she lost, it's so hard to imagine how happy she was all the time. Just to be alive, she loved life, loved everyone around her. A trait my father shared deep in his core, but hated to admit to.

Matthew takes a seat next to me at the long, sleek marble bar while Olivia flits around the kitchen before us, arranging the ravioli and other snacks.

"I know this waiting has been torture for you, Sophie, and you have just been through so much in the last few months. I feel like I have missed it all. I haven't been there for you like I should, and I need to check in with you and make sure you are ok. Are you…ok?" She stops and looks at me picking up a jar of wine, waiting for my prompt.

"I will be," I return softly as we toast and each silently sip our pleasantly cheap red wine.

"Oh this reminds me of your Lola," a cherubic grin spreads across Olivia's rosy cheeks. "God, I loved her. She was so much better than both of my grandmothers."

"Tell me about your grandma, Sophie," says Matthew as he pops an olive into his mouth.

"Oh, Matthew, you would have loved Lola. She drank her wine from the jug." Olivia raises her glass in toast to me before continuing. "She did not stand on ceremony, like my stuffy-ass grandparents, unless there was a saint to be worshipped."

"Wine started after coffee," I interject with a wink, taking a slug of my wine. "She taught me to cook, and drink, and pray." I empty my glass and choke on a chuckle as I remember one of her many sayings. She always has a tid bit of wisdom usually pertaining to drinking and praying that would apply to any and every situation.

"You must learn to carry the guilt in your heart, it frees up your hands for bread and wine."

"Interesting life philosophy," says Matthew.

"It was the pride of being Italian. She would say, 'God's chosen people. Why else would the Pope, God save his soul," Olivia and I both do the sign of the Trinity across our chests with a giggle and a nod, "live in Rome? Italians can pray with a sausage in their mouths and a glass of wine in their hands."

"She made me want to be Italian. I was always so envious of your Lola, Sophie."

"I know!" I exclaim and stick my tongue out at her. "She was the best. I am really going to miss her." A heavy moment passes over us but doesn't last long. She wouldn't have wanted that; she would hate for us to be sad. She would want us to drink and eat and laugh, and Olivia knows this well. She pulls a loaf of bread from the oven with a bubbling cauldron of artichoke fondue, one of Lola's favorite recipes.

We eat, drink and tell stories until early in the morning and it is cathartic and therapeutic, and for a fleeting moment I almost forget that Rhys is laying in the hospital, in a coma, and I can't get near him.

I'm able to force myself into a short two hours of sleep before I can't fake it anymore. The dawn is barely breaking, the smog filled New York skyline glows a pearly pink while people begin to move. Garbage trucks and street sweepers dot the street below and the bakery on the corner is lit up and already bustling. The thought of Rhys lying there alone tortures me, takes over my mind, consumes my thoughts, and clouds my vision. A walk, a walk will clear my head. I know I will see him soon, today maybe. Matthew says I must be patient. Bianca is on the war path, and I am not family.

CH. 4

The dark tower rising into the early morning water color clouds called to me and I couldn't think of anything else. I had left with the intention of a mind clearing walk. The fact that my feet took me the twenty-three blocks to the hospital in the darkest hours of the dawn couldn't be helped. Before I had made the conscious choice, I was already walking through the sliding doors. The smell of antiseptic and floor polish hit me like a ton of bricks and a slow panic begins to creep.

A quick smile to the elderly woman behind the information desk and I check the directory for the ICU and wait for the elevator. *Tap, tap, tap.* My foot taps unbidden on the cold tile floor, echoing across the small corridor that houses a large bank of elevators. The elevator crawls torturously, allowing too much time for my anxiety to rise and reason to creep in. When the doors open on the ICU floor, the desk is deserted, the lights are low, and it is quiet, except for the rhythmic chirping of the various life support machines. There is a half circle of rooms that surround the desk, each with its own sliding glass doors.

The faint light from machines cast shadows around the ward, and there he lies in the first cubicle, his messy dark hair the giveaway. I forget to breathe and my chest constricts around my beating heart. He is still while the machines rattle on, his skin is looks pale and ashen, his limbs lifeless. My heart drops like a rock and I fight back a curtain of tears, wanting so badly to rush to him. A glass door slides open and I duck around the corner, down an empty hallway unsure of what I'm hiding from, but unable to walk boldly to Rhys' side. He looks so unreal, like a nightmare, a hallucination.

I hear the elevators open and three voices emerge; one slow and soothing, one high and shrill, the other filled with grief.

"It appears that the swelling has begun to recede which is good, as long as he continues to make progress they will want to wake him up as soon as possible. The swelling is the main concern for us at this point, but we will know more tomorrow. There is really nothing more we can do but observe him. Now, you really should go home and get some rest." I watch the shadow of the nurse stretch and disappear before the voices continue.

"He can't leave me like this, Bianca. He just can't."

"Don't you worry, Mon Cher. I'm sure he will pull through, you'll see. You tell him about that baby and my Rhys will pull through. That's just the kind of man he is."

In the blink of an eye a series of events is unleashed completely beyond my control or comprehension. My heart leaps into my throat and I choke and cough on Bianca's words. Nadja turns in a whirl of blonde hair and running mascara. Bianca's eyes almost pop from her head before she shrieks.

"Nurse!" At the top of her lungs, she raises the alarm. "Nurse! Nurse! Where is the fucking nurse?" The French bend in her words makes her sound oddly elegant as she shrieks like a lunatic. She turns and slaps the countertop of the empty nurses' station. "This woman is trespassing and harassing my family! Where is a goddamn nurse?"

Two nurses emerge from behind a sliding glass door as a security guard appears swiftly from around the corner. Bianca is on him in an instant before I can even take a second breath.

"This girl does not belong here and is not welcome. I want her removed from this ward and kept away from my son. Do you understand?" Wagging her finger in the guard's face, she turns to the nurses. "Did you hear me?" she demands, her shrill voice bouncing from the cold hard floor, filling the ICU with her desperate anger.

"Yes, Mrs. Slate. Now please lower your voice, ma'am. There are patients sleeping." The brave nurse steps forward before Bianca cuts her off. "Do not tell me to lower my voice. I want this person removed and I want it done now. My son is lying in that room, clinging to life! She is no friend of his and certainly not part of this family. My husband contributes a substantial amount of money to this hospital and I want her removed. So remove her." With every word her tone becomes calmer, and ever more menacing. She has found her power. The nurses' eyes bulge as they look to each other for guidance before the guard grabs me by the arm.

"Come with me." I look down at his large, calloused hand around my arm, and then up into his tired, confused eyes. An apology is evident as is a healthy fear that drives him to push me towards the elevator. As the doors open and he leads me in, I hear Bianca.

"You are to make sure she does not return. I don't want her anywhere near my son." The elevator doors slide closed and I fear I may never see Rhys again.

Twenty-four hours later all I can hear are Bianca's words bouncing around my head. *"You tell him about that baby and my Rhys will pull through."* I have been trapped in my own personal hell; one more minute will drive me insane. As I stare down into my phone, scrolling through contacts, lost as to what I should be doing, I see Nina's number, his gate keeper, if anyone knows anything, it would be her. I scroll back and think twice before dropping my phone and running to Olivia's room.

"Liv, I need to talk to you." She is perched up in her bed watching Bravo, computer in her lap, phone in her hand, and Bluetooth in her ear.

"Come in, sweetie, I'm so glad you are finally up." She takes the Bluetooth from her ear and closes her laptop, pushing it away from her. I climb into her plush bed next to her.

"I wasn't sleeping."

"You have been so quiet, Sophie. What have you been doing? I miss you, talk to me." She silences her phone before placing it on the bedside table and I sidle up next to her, resting my head on her shoulder.

"I did something, Liv." She just watches me, waiting for me to continue. "I went to the hospital early yesterday morning."

"Did you see him?" she asks as she plays with my hair.

"You aren't mad?"

"Sophie, of course I'm not mad, sweetie. I'm surprised it took you this long, to be honest. I half expected you to jump out of the car that first day. I know Matthew has been a bit of a stickler, but he really is just looking out for you. It would not be good if you ran into Bianca, trust me."

"Well," I sit up and turn towards her, my head hanging, my eyes barely meeting hers, "she was there and she had me kicked out of the hospital and banned." The reality of the moment, what I heard, and the memory of his broken form converge and I can no longer hold back the tears. A soft shower of salty sorrow falls across my face and my voice breaks. Olivia just rubs my back and waits for me to catch my breath all the while whispering to me how sorry she is, cursing Bianca under her breath.

"That's not the worst," I say, shifting out from under her hands. I have to face this moment head on. There is no hiding from it, and quite frankly her reaction will tell me more than anything at this point. If what Bianca said about a baby is true, could possibly be true, Olivia will surely know and she won't be able to hide it from me; and if she doesn't, she will know just who we need to go to.

"What could be worse than Bianca throwing you out of the hospital?" she asks, her forehead crinkled in confusion. I take a deep breath and prepare myself for a reality that will change everything. A horrible truth, I fear with every fiber of my being she will confirm. "What is it, Sophie?"

A flood gate bursts and waves of information pour forth; tales of his mother screaming like a lunatic, the sound of her shrill voice bouncing from the stark walls, the monotonous rhythm of the machines playing a sad lament, the mortified nurse and Nadja's tear stained cheeks, every last detail, until I'm blue in the face and have to stop to take a breath. Olivia's face is frozen motionless for a split second before I watch every word slowly register and a fire grow behind her eyes.

"Are you fucking kidding me right now? No.

Just, no, that…No. She cannot be pregnant. Not by Rhys, Sophie, that is just too convenient and total bullshit. No." She grabs her phone and scrolls. I smile unable to do much else, overwhelmed by putting words to my pain, but totally in awe of her determined response. She takes a deep breath and looks me in the eye, centering herself, centering me. "I'm sorry, Sophie," she takes my hand in hers, "I'm so sorry that all of this is happening, that the world seems to be just…shitting all over you right now. But, this…this cannot be true. You have to know that. Do you believe me? I don't believe it. We are going to get to the bottom of this, and we will start with Nina."

"Yes," she taps her phone and it begins to ring, "Rhys is far from perfect, Sophie." She looks me in the eye demanding my attention, "far from perfect." She nods as if to affirm that I understand. "But that man is lost for you, he has talked of nothing else. He has not been with Nadja and she is just crazy enough to try something like this when he is unable to answer for himself. It's uncanny timing, and I just refuse to believe it. You should do the same."

Nina's phone goes straight to voicemail.

"Nina, this is Olivia. I am sitting here with Sophie. Please call me back as soon as possible. It's an emergency."

"An emergency?" I question, unsure I'm ready to open what could be a can of worms.

"Fuck, yes, it's an emergency. My girl's heart is breaking and I mean to fix it. Now, Sophie, let's talk about what we do know, what you know." My heart sinks at her tone, her '*I'm about to hurt you with some truth*' tone.

"All I know is what happened between them before I left. I assume…or assumed that he hadn't seen her again. Now, I'm afraid I was wrong." I take a pensive breath and gird myself, "What do you know, Olivia? What have I missed…again?"

"No, Sophie. It's not like that. At least, I don't think so." A familiar look of pity briefly passes across her eyes and I hate it, I hate being back here in this moment, this limbo of not knowing, not understanding what has happened, or the consequences it will bring upon me.

"I know that he spent the weekend in the Hamptons earlier this month, and I'm pretty sure she was there." I cringe at the thought as she continues, her voice drifting as if she is whispering to herself. "I don't understand why Kylie can't see her for what she is. She opened the door this time, and, of course, Nadja just lit it all on fire!" She rests her head in her hands and sighs, frustration seeping from every pore.

"He went away with her?" It takes a moment for the thought to register, for my mind to accept what she said. And then the buzz, roaring, white noise fills my head and my blood boils, but before I can wander too far down angers dark path, Olivia stops me.

"No! He didn't *'go away'* with her; he went to the Hamptons with his family. Kylie brought Nadja along, if I understand correctly."

"Why? Why would she do that? Did he know that she was going to be there? This is all so fucked up, Olivia. I don't know how much more I can take." I refuse to fucking cry, instead holding in my breath until the tears pass. "I feel like my heart is shredded." I drop my head into my hands and close my eyes. "This can't be happening. I don't know if I can go through this again." My voice is hushed and I'm barely aware that Olivia can even hear me. All I can hear is the pounding of my own heart and the sound of being alone.

"Let's not jump to any conclusions, Sophie. You've held on this long, you can hang in there just a bit longer until we find out the truth. I know there has to be an explanation for all of this." She grabs my hands and centers her attention on me. "In all the time I have known Rhys, I have never known him to be so distracted. He has never been one to easily have his head turned, Sophie, but you have taken over this man's thoughts. I swear he never talks about anything else. It's so damned annoying." She smiles and I laugh, unable to fight her charm or the memories. I will cling to the words we have shared, the moments we made, and the promises he has made to me. I will cling to his words and his actions and not let the doubt and manipulations of Nadja seep in and make me forget.

"In all seriousness, Sophie, I think he loves you." She beams with a secondhand pride and waits. I get lost in the thought, recalling that moment when he blurted over the phone those three little words. I can't imagine that's how he meant to deliver them, but I couldn't have cared less about the scene or the fact we were on the phone; the sound of his voice saying those words to me, the sincerity and utter conviction, the need. I love him. I knew I loved him the moment I left him. I knew I needed him the moment Olivia told me I might lose him.

"I know he loves me." When I finally say it, the words take flight like a million fireflies and illuminate everything around me; clarity, finally.

Her face lights up and she crouches closer to me, gossip stance, head tilted slightly to the left, eyes wide in anticipation of some juicy news.

"Has he already told you he loves you? And you didn't tell me?"

"He has," I return with a coy smile and a sigh, "the day of the accident. He called me that morning and asked me to come back."

"That is unreal, Sophie, did you say it back?" she asks with baited breath.

"Of course I said it back, are you kidding?" I

fill my chest with breath and continue while she smiles like an idiot. "Of course, I love him, Olivia. How could I not?"

"Well," she starts as she hops off the bed, "I knew you loved him. I just wasn't sure you knew it yet." She turns and looks at me with a sly grin, knowing how reluctant I have always been to confess my feelings. When you open your heart and admit to your feelings for someone, you become beholden to those feelings, a slave to those feelings. I've been a slave to infatuation and irrational attachment. I won't go back. I am saved from any further probing by the ring of her phone. She sprints across the room to catch it.

"Yes!" she exclaims, holding it up before she answers. "It's Nina." She paces back and forth across the hallway, throwing me a wink and a thumbs up every once in a while. Disappearing behind a closed door, she tries to dig deeper. She volleys calls between Kylie and Nina until she is satisfied that she has pieced together a story.

By the next morning, Olivia has managed to crack the code. We walk and talk and she fills me in on every little sordid and calculated detail. Nadja's twisted sense of loyalty and betrayal is beyond me. She used Kylie, broke her heart and blamed her for it, claiming it was all in the name of love. Then just as quickly as she arrived, she disappears for two days and shows up with her ex.

It took hours for Kylie to crack, she was so humiliated and hurt, but she and Olivia had once been close, I knew she would get it out of her eventually. The way Nadja led her on is sickening, her claims of wanting to protect Rhys from embarrassment and ruin were just a Band-Aid to Kylie's aching heart. She lied to Kylie, she lied to Bianca, she lied to everyone.

Olivia concludes that the baby must belong to the ex, but I'm not so sure. I'm not sure there is a baby at all, but only time will tell. I can't imagine the turmoil this would all be causing Rhys. Part of me wishes he was here to help me through, yet another part is relieved that he is not so we can figure all this out without his interference, without him 'protecting' me by keeping it all away from me. Olivia hits the shower in triumph while I pace the kitchen and process

"Sophie!" I hear the door swing open and Matthew's heavy footsteps as he bounds through the foyer. I catch him coming around the corner, winded, but a positive grin on his face. "Sophie," he stops to catch his breath and rests his hands on my shoulders, centering himself, focusing on me. "Sophie, Michael asked for you." As his words sink in, my heart leaps into my throat and I tear up the stairs and into my room, grabbing my purse and rushing out the door, hot on Matthews heels. I am overwhelmed with glee at the idea of being even in the same building as Rhys.

When I walk into Michael's room the strangest sense of relief crashes over me, wave after wave, until I am a sobbing, soggy mess. Anyone witnessing the ordeal would believe I had walked into my own father's room to discover him alive and well, just a little worse for wear, but this isn't my father; this is Michael Slate, *the* Michael Slate, and he summoned me. I stand at the door, unable to move, unsure of what to do, and mortified by my emotional outburst over this man I have met but once for just a moment.

"My goodness, young lady, why do you weep like that?" He motions for me to come closer.

"I...I'm sorry, Mr. Slate, I am just so glad to see you, happy that you are okay." My voice cracks as I wipe away tears, trying to clear my vision.

"Dear sweet girl, no wonder my son has fallen so hard for you. Come in and sit, Sophie, we have a few things to discuss."

"Discuss?" I question, pulling a chair up to his bedside. There is something so familiar about this man, so gentle, he puts me right at ease, although I can't fathom what we could have to discuss. "Shouldn't you rest?"

"No, my dear girl, I have been doing nothing but resting due to these militant nurses." He winks at the short Latina nurse who is checking his IV and she blushes deeply, fluttering her eyelashes at him before leaving the room, leaving us alone. "Now, I assume you have seen my son?"

"No, sir."

"No?" The shock in his voice echoes from the cold hospital walls. "How is it possible that you haven't seen him yet?"

I pause for a moment, remembering what Rhys has told me about his mother and father, wondering if it is a good idea to even bring her up.

"Well, um….," I struggle to find my voice, "Bianca."

"Bianca, of course. Say no more, Sophie, say no more." He shakes his head and reaches to his bedside table, grabbing a pair of readers and a small stack of papers. "Don't you worry about Bianca anymore, young lady, we will rectify this immediately. I was able to see him for a bit this morning. The boy is being quite lazy if you ask me. Always with the dramatics." He looks over his glasses with a wink and a crinkled nose. "I've been told the swelling has subsided so they will be taking him off of those God awful drugs. He should be back to himself in no time"

I am amazed that he can have a sense of humor, lying in a hospital bed while his son hovers precariously in a coma; yet I am completely overwhelmed and distracted by the idea of finally being able to see Rhys, my heart could burst, yet, it is fear that chokes me. What will he look like? God,

I don't want to cry, but I already feel the tears sneaking in. Every fear from the last few days comes rushing in and I am drowning in 'what if's?' When I look up, I see Mr. Slate's questioning face.

"I'm sorry, I didn't hear you," I mumble, trapped in my own mind. I barely make eye contact and he just grins.

"It's quite alright, my dear, I didn't say a word. I was just watching you, admiring you. My son has told me so much about you, I feel like we are old friends, or family, perhaps." My chest warms at his words and my heart swells, pushing a heavy tear down my cheek. "I think you should take some time to go see him first. We can talk when you return. Call the nurse for me and we'll get someone to accompany you to make sure there aren't any misunderstandings."

CH. 5

The wind is knocked from my lungs when I step into his darkened room. His skin is cool and tacky. Limp fingers splay from his open hand; his arms lay lifeless at his sides. Machines pump blood into his body, oxygen into his lungs, and life into his heart. His full lips are slack and gray, desperate for the heat of a kiss to wake him from his slumber. I lean over and kiss him gently, careful not to disturb the breathing tube, but his mouth is hard and unresponsive. Like a fool in a fairy tale, I step back for a moment, hoping for him to wake up, but he just lies there.

The heart monitor doesn't skip a beat, not even a flutter. I slide my fingers into his open hand and squeeze, setting a slow, pulsing rhythm like the beat of a heart, squeezing his hand and releasing; my own life support, something to distract me from the silence, the crushing lack of his voice that scares me and takes me to a place I do not want to be. The place where I am alone, no family, no heart; that's about as alone as it gets.

I must have sat there just watching his chest rise and fall for over an hour, the stagnant beat of the machines lulling me into a state of hypnosis. I breathe in when he inhales, and I exhale with him. His breaths are shallow, but getting deeper with every pull.

"You will not leave me alone, do you hear

me?" I rest my arms on the bed and lean into him. He does not smell like my Rhys. He smells like antiseptic and fresh plastic. Just a hint of his rosemary and mint shampoo remains behind his ear, and I take a deep hit, pulling him as far into my lungs as I can.

"Leave it to you to do something so dramatic just to get me back here. Everything has to be big with you, always showing off." I lay my head down on the bed next to our entwined hands and take a deep breath, cooling my throat. "You have my attention now. I am sorry that I left, that I didn't stay and just tell you the truth. I wish that I could do that now. Do you even know I am here? Do you want me here?" His pinky flutters. *Did I feel that? Did I make it up*? An almost imperceptible squeeze from all fingers makes my heart pound.

"Do that again," I quietly demand. His fingers tighten around mine and my heart leaps into my throat. A violent tattoo thumps against my chest. I pick up his call button and ring for the nurse. His head rolls to the side and a gentle flutter crosses the dark lashes that lay on his cheek. He squeezes my hand again. I grasp him so strongly wanting to give him strength, my strength. The nurses rush into the room and shoo me away from his bed, ripping him from my grip as they check his machines and talk to him. His eyes flutter, but don't open.

"Mr. Slate, can you open your eyes?" the nurse

asks, checking his pulse. "Mr. Slate, do you know where you are?" I watch as his head rolls and his beautiful green eyes open. He looks right at me and my heart stops. A small smile cracks across his stiff mouth and I stop breathing for a moment. Dropping my shoulders, I can finally breathe deeply and a sigh of relief starts deep in my toes. He tries to talk, but the breathing tube down his throat won't allow it. One of the nurses turns to me and herds me towards the door.

"I need you to step outside, miss."

"But," my tongue is twisted and the thought of leaving his side is atrocious.

"It will only be a few moments. Just so we can remove his breathing tube and check his vitals. Just wait right outside, I'll come get you." She gently nudges me out the door and closes it behind her, and I wait. After what feels like an hour, although, I'm sure it was maybe five minutes, the door opens and I walk back into the room, watching as a nurse hands him a cup of ice chips. Slowly they make their way from the room, one by one. When we are alone again, he is lying with his eyes closed and I am anchored to the corner, wondering if it was all a dream.

"Sophie," his hoarse voice pulls me from my shock and I rush to his side, sweeping his hand into mine. I caress the back of his hand with my damp cheek. My heart full of relief, but fractured from such intense worry. It aches in my chest, threatening to burst. I climb onto the narrow hospital bed and I curl around him, my head resting on his chest. The thump of his heart against my ear is magical and the feel of his warm breath sliding down my neck has me floating. We have another chance. I get another chance. I look up into his face and find his eyes wide and warm. Dark circles cast a shadow down his cheek and his jaw is covered by a faint beard.

"You scared me," I whisper.

"I had to get you back here," he teases, pulling me closer. His grasp is weak, so I press myself against him. The nurses don't let me linger for long, and he isn't awake for more than a few minutes before the exhaustion and residual drugs take him back into a deep sleep but, my heart is lighter for the few moments we have.

When I return to Michael's room, he appears to be asleep, but as I try to duck out quietly he sits up with a sly grin.

"Don't go, Ms. Noelle," he chuckles, "I was just playing possum. The nurse keeps trying to give me a sponge bath and she just won't take no for an answer." He winks at me and I burst into laughter, over tired, delirious laughter that catches me off guard, but makes him chuckle with pride at his joke.

"I see what my boy likes about you, my dear, that smile is enough to light the night." I feel myself turn crimson and bite back my laughter out of embarrassment. "Don't stifle that enchanting sound; it makes me feel young to make a beautiful woman laugh." I smile at him and take a seat next to the bed.

"You sell yourself short, Mr. Slate," I tease as he pulls a stack of papers into his lap and slides on his bi-focals.

"Please, no formalities. I want you to call me Michael." He looks over the rim of his glasses and waits for me to agree.

"Yes, sir," I remark, without thinking.

"Sir? Now you are laboring to make me feel old again, young lady." I open my mouth, but not a word slips out. "Relax, I'm teasing. You're adorable when you blush." I sit back and try to fight off the red as he shuffles the papers in his lap. "Now, it has occurred to me that my son will want to go over most of this with you, but there is one caveat that I would like to address. Whereas, I would seldom doubt his judgment when it comes to matters of business, I always do my due diligence."

"I'm not sure I understand what we are talking about."

"My son let a very valuable piece of property go after you left; a piece of property that he had fought hard to keep, most notably against my wishes. I have a keen sense that you had something to do with that."

"I'm not following you, sir, I'm sorry."

"A charitable trust was set up in your name, Ms. Noelle. An educational trust, and its first rule of business was to save PS138. Rhys had invested in a very restricted piece of property directly adjacent to the school, one he had planned to develop against stiff opposition from the community and the school board. He was working to have that school shut down to clear the way for his development."

"I know what you're talking about, but I don't understand what it has to do with me?"

"It has everything to do with you, my dear. I had been urging him for over a year to let that property go, to donate it and move on, but he had his heels dug so far into the dirt there was no moving him. He is a shrewd business man, but has always been better than me at leaving his heart at the door. Emotional decisions are not his style; this was most definitely an emotional decision. And, as it is the decision I was always hoping he would come to, I have to ask myself, why?" I don't know what to say. He shot me down and barely listened to me that night. I surely had nothing to do with that decision. "Now, it's quite obvious that he is taken with you, I thought it only proper that we get to know each other better since we will inevitably be working together."

"Now, I'm sure I don't know what you're talking about."

"No, you wouldn't, but you will. And in any

case, that's not important now. What is important, Sophie, is how you feel about Rhys. I think I can guess." I am stunned into silence, not sure what he is asking or what he wants. "He loves you." He watches my reaction closely, but there is no surprise, just a wash of comfort in hearing someone else's utterance of the words. "I don't know that he had a chance to tell you, but he does."

"Yes, sir, he did" my voice cracks slightly and look into his eyes and letting the moment stretch.

"I see. Well, thank the good Lord for that then. I do believe the man upstairs was looking after us that day. He will be ok, you know. He has a few battered bones and a few other minor scrapes, but he will be ok. It is just that brain they are worried about, but he will be ok, just as I will be, just as we all will be." My chest swells at the familiar way he addresses me, as if we truly are family.

After a long, awkward conversation full of questions, but no direct answers, I am still left in the dark, feeling as if I have passed some test set forth by Michael. I can't believe Rhys gave that land back. I'm so very proud of him. I ask Michael to make sure I can stay the night with Rhys and call Olivia to have her bring me some things. There is no way I am leaving his side again, not until we can walk out of this hospital together.

CH. 6

The first restful sleep I have had in weeks and I wake with a stiff neck and a wet cheek stuck to the mattress. As I lift my weary head I see his shining eyes staring back at me. I quickly wipe the drool from my mouth, *how embarrassing.* His eyes twinkle and he wrinkles his nose, watching me stretch and wake, but there is sadness etched in the lines of his face, a sadness I do not understand. He looks as if he has something stuck on the end of his tongue. He opens his mouth, but before he can speak the nurse throws back the sliding door and starts rustling machines about.

"Good morning, Mr. Slate. Glad to see you finally have decided to join us, we were wondering when you were going to wake from that beauty rest." She winks at me as she takes his blood pressure and reads the monitors. "Everything is looking good so far here. I think a bit of breakfast would do you well, so I'll be right back with a tray." She is in and out of the room before either of us can get a word in and suddenly we are left…alone.

It's an odd sensation this morning in this room with him. I can't put my finger on it, but something is just not right, and as I look into his eyes I know he feels it too. He is watching me as if it may be the last time, like he is trying to take it all in, commit me to memory. My heart thumps in my chest as a familiar anxiety takes hold, only to be confirmed by his deep, soul wrenching sigh as he pats the bedside.

"Come here, Sophie, we need to talk." I hate those words, and suddenly I want to sprint from the room, to run out of earshot before he has a chance to say whatever it is he is about to say, to flee this impending…whatever it is. I know we have to do this but I just don't want to. I didn't come all this way to be hurt again, but before I can put tread to the floor, my stupid heart drives me towards the bedside and I climb up next to him, a pensive feeling in my heart. As I gain the courage to look up into his eyes, he is shaking his head at me, at war with himself and I cannot take it.

"I think I know what you are going to say," I blurt out, pushing away from him, inching closer and closer to the edge with every passing silent second

"Sophie, I meant what I said. I love you." He takes my hands into his, his fingers caressing my palms, lulling me into a false security. "But something happened after you left. Something you have to know about." And with each syllable my heart starts to harden, a defense mechanism, my only protection. I don't say a word as I listen to his breathing, labored, deep and deliberate, and to his heart monitor as it steadily grows in rhythm.

"I am far from perfect, Sophie, far, far from it.

You know this already. I try and I will try harder. I will move mountains to be worthy of you." His eyes are cast away from mine as he caresses the back of my hands with a hypnotic beat. "I need you to love me back, Sophie. I need it like air." God, he is killing me and I almost think to tell him I know. *Almost.* This may be my only chance to hear his side of the story and I cruelly decide to let him sweat it out just a little bit longer.

"Sophie, with you I know exactly who and what I want to be, and I have a lot of work to do. I just hope that you can find it in your heart to give me another chance, but I fear you will not." My blood begins to turn to ice, slowing in my veins, throbbing under my skin. My mind struggles to throw back up those walls that he had so easily toppled before he proceeds to crush me with whatever he is about to say. He winces as he tries to sit up and I look at him, broken and battered, and can't take another minute.

"I know about the Hamptons, Rhys. I know about Nadja." The words fall from my mouth like the water over Angel Falls and he is stunned.

"What?" He turns, mouth gaping, worry etched into his forehead. "But, how could you?" I watch him for a split second angrily muse to himself about Nadja and her evil spirit. When he finally stops, I look into his eyes and see a broken man, just how she wanted him.

"I am sorry, Sophie. Never, ever did I think I was capable of such a thing, and after what you have been through, I would not blame you if you could never forgive me. How did you find out?" he asks in a hoarse whisper, barely making eye contact.

"I overheard her and your mother talking."

"She told my mother?"

"Of course, she told your mother. That was all part of her plan, I imagine." The corners of his eyes crinkle in question.

"What do you mean her plan?"

"I imagine it was all a ploy to get you back, or at least to drive me away and to bring your mother under her thumb."

"I don't understand, Sophie. What are we talking about here?" He grabs for the remote and adjusts the bed until he is sitting straight upright.

"What are you talking about?" I ask him, more confused than ever, unable to decipher between the two of us what is actually being said. "I heard your mother and Nadja talking, Rhys, about a baby."

"Whose baby?" He goes white as a ghost and it hits me. He has no idea what I'm talking about. Then, what the hell is he talking about? I take a breath; pausing a beat in an attempt to measure my words, but there is no way around it. This is not going to be good. I gird myself and steady my voice.

"She claims that it is your baby." Atom bombs

ignite behind his eyes and I see the mushrooming anger overtake him. His pulse spikes, the monitors start going nuts and two nurses rush into the room, pushing me into the corner.

"Mr. Slate, you'll need to calm down!"

I watch one of them empty a syringe into his IV as the monitors calm and he sinks back amongst the pillows, the anger still etched into his face, but his body relaxed against his will.

"Please, Mr. Slate, it is vital that you remain calm." She turns to me, "And you, Miss, it is important for Mr. Slate's recovery that he doesn't get worked up. Perhaps you should go and let him rest."

"No!" he barks, struggling to sit back up. "No, I want her to stay. I want you to go," he says, nodding towards the door.

"Ok, Mr. Slate, but you must remain in bed, sir, and remain calm." As the nurses exit the room, he nods towards the slider door.

"Close the door, Sophie. I slowly move across the room and slide the door shut while he sits up, watching my every move. When I return to the bedside, I pull up a chair and sit down, waiting.

"My baby," he hisses cold and distant, he looks into me, his eyes narrow and half sleepy. "Do you think it's my baby?" his mouth begging the question.

"No." And as I say it, I know in my heart, it's

true; not after seeing her with that man, not after everything she has done thus far. No. No, I don't believe a word that woman says, and just like that I am resolved. Looking into his eyes, I see the gratitude, the sheer relief. "I don't believe a word she says." He sinks back into the bed with a sigh of relief.

"Sophie, I swear I haven't laid a hand on her in over six months, maybe longer" he stops and ponders something for a moment, "well...not in that way." His face twists in a mask of disgust and he won't meet my eyes.

"Sophie..," his voice is strained, quiet, "I don't know..." He stops mid-sentence, shaking his head, looking so forlorn, so torn. I'm begging to speak, but he stops me. "Sophie, I hit her. I mean, I think I hit her."

"What?" Stunned, I stare at him, unable to see the person who would do such a thing.

"In the Hamptons, Nadja was there as Kylie's guest." I sink back into the chair, blood pressure already rising, trying to hide my growing fear.

"I know about the Hamptons," I interrupt, not wanting to rehash the details, but he just keeps going.

"I had too much to drink and let my guard down and, well...." I close my eyes and take a breath, filling my lungs before my head is filled with the worst possible thoughts. "I don't remember it, and I know that is no excuse. But she showed up at my office that Monday after the Hamptons with a black eye and a split lip." I watch his lips move, but can't hear a word he is saying. A fuzzy white noise fills my ears and I feel like I'm drowning in static. "She was in the pool house. I remember that…I think. We shared a drink; I'm sure, and then…nothing."

Could it be the hands that caressed my skin, the fingers that healed my heart, and the lips that kissed my pain away, could he really be the same monster? Even as I look at him, watch him, listen to him confess, I cannot believe what he is saying. Never, never would I think that he was capable of such a thing. But his lips don't lie, the pain in his eyes isn't a lie, the guilt that mars his beautiful face cannot be wrong.

My heart sinks to the cold hard ground and a terrible hole sits between us, heavy and rife with despair. It is palpable, the shame rolling off of him, the dismay that surrounds me, and we sit in silence, a cold heavy silence. My mind races replaying every lovely thing he has ever said to me, every word about my worth, about Collin's cowardice. It doesn't add up and then Nadja pops into my head; visions of her suspended against the wall by that brute and suddenly I am overcome. My mind refuses to accept that he would do such a thing, and a startling clarity crashes over me like a wave that knocks me down and steals my breath, sending me tumbling through the surf until I emerge with an entirely different perspective.

It all starts to make sense. Blocks of information bouncing around in my head, coming together to form a more complete picture, a picture of desperate manipulation and unfortunate misunderstandings, assumptions and accusations, none of which holds any weight. When the pieces align, it becomes infinitely clear. I look into his eyes with more determination and clarity than I have felt in ages, and as guilt mars his face, triumph fills my heart. It all makes sense, twisted sick sense. Clearing the fog, I begin to work it out, out loud.

"I saw her the first time I tried to visit you, with a man. It was so odd; I didn't know what to do." I shake my head and let the remaining pieces fall into place while Rhys watches curiously. "He put his hand on her belly, how could I have missed that?"

"Sophie, what the hell are you talking about?" I just look at him blank and it all falls into place.

"I have to call Olivia."

"First, you have to tell me what you are talking about, please! I am totally lost." His eyes plead for my response as I furiously type out a text to Olivia. I take a deep breath and center myself before launching into my hypothesis.

"I don't know for sure, Rhys, but I can't believe that you would hurt her, that she would allow you to hurt her. When I heard her say she was pregnant, I was stunned. I told Olivia and she got pissed, insisting it was not possible."

"It's not possible, I swear it."

"I know, Rhys, I believe you." I kiss the back of his hand and sit on the edge of the bed. "Olivia wasted no time once I told her. She called Nina right away and had her run down your personal schedule. Nina confirmed that it wasn't possible, that you hadn't even seen one another until the wedding, Nadja was not even in the country at the time she would have conceived."

"Thank God, Sophie. I swear I would never, ever do that to you."

"Rhys, she saw an opportunity and jumped; you got hurt, the coma, it all worked out so perfectly for her, but she wasn't banking on me coming back, on Olivia calling her bluff. I had bits and pieces of information, but it didn't fit together until now. Your mother was keeping me away." He waits with baited breath while I spin the tale. "I saw her, Rhys, with a man in the alley just outside. They were clearly…involved, but he was being very rough with her, I mean really rough. He choked her and held her against the wall. I have no idea what he was saying, but I'd bet it was threatening. Yet, in the very next breath they embraced. He put his hand on her belly, Rhys, like an expectant father would." He sits back against the pillows and struggles for a deep breath.

"Sergei."

"Who is Sergei?"

"Nadja's ex-husband."

"Is he a violent man?"

"That's a bit of an understatement," he scoffs, adjusting himself, pressing the call button for the nurse.

"What can I get you, Rhys, let me help."

"I need to see my father, Sophie." When the nurse comes in, he asks to see Michael. She scurries off to find a wheel chair while we wait in virtual silence and Rhys quietly seethes. "I can't believe she would do this." It's barely a whisper, and not meant for my ears. I just hold his hand and wait for the nurse to return. When someone finally arrives with a wheelchair, it takes them a while to get him out of bed and into the chair, an IV pole trailing behind him. I hop up to follow them and he stops me dead in my tracks. "No, Sophie, you stay here." My heart sinks, making it impossible to hide the hurt on my face. He reaches out to take my hand. "Trust me, please."

A deep, discontented sigh rips from my lungs yet I agree under duress, tired of being left out, weary of always being asked to just trust. I am tired of this woman pulling the strings of my life, doing everything in her power to make me miserable, to make Rhys miserable. I want to rip her to shreds, to

scream at the top of my lungs, *'What the FUCK!'*
Instead, I muster a disingenuous smile and sit back
down on the hard hospital chair and wait.

Ch. 7

Unable to find the television remote, I doze off in the chair watching some Spanish language soap opera. When he returns, he wakes me softly with a kiss to the back of the hand before they help him back into bed and get him hooked up to his monitors. He seems more at peace, but tight lipped. I decide I have had enough for one day and resolve not to bring her up again until I have the energy to deal with her madness.

"Dr. Holder will be in in the morning, Mr. Slate, to check your status."

"When will I be discharged?"

"We need to observe you for a few days at least, I wouldn't get too anxious. We will have to wait and see what the doctor says, I would make myself comfortable if I were you. You've been through quite an ordeal, we want you whole and well. Now, I will be back in a couple of hours to check your vitals and assess your pain." She slides the glass door shut and we are alone again.

"Thank you for understanding, Sophie. I had to talk with my father to make sure we are safe to cut ties with Viktor once and for all, and by extension, Nadja. It's going to be a delicate thing to extract her from our foundations and make it look like her choice. I need her to step down. I just have to make sure everything else is in place. I promise, Sophie, I won't let her hurt us anymore. This is the last straw for her and me. I mean to untangle once and for all and make a clean break that she has no choice but to accept."

"How are you planning to do that?" He taps his temple with a sly grin across his lips.

"Always working, baby, remember? I have been formulating a plan for a while, my father has wanted to extricate from Viktor. The more we got into his business, the more we realized why he was going under. There is no oversight, and he has dealings with some very shady characters, Sergei being one of them. We had been visiting all of his various holdings around the city, empty warehouses and storage facilities that he couldn't account for.

The day we were in the accident, I thought I saw Sergei, but the connection didn't make sense and I let it go, but in light of what you've told me, I can no longer turn a blind eye. If Nadja is mixed up with Sergei again, there is no helping her. If we can only get her to move on, to resign, and allow her to believe that it was all her idea."

"Why on earth would she agree or go along with anything like that? She has been fighting so hard to get you back?"

"We play on her vanity, my love. It's her Achilles' heel and it's time to hit her where it hurts."

"You are positively glowing with deviousness, Mr. Slate." The blush in his cheeks is brighter than it has been and there is a genuine gleam in his eyes.

"Close the curtain, Sophie, and come here." I slide the curtain across the door and climb onto the narrow hospital bed. "You have changed my life, Sophie. I don't know what I've done to deserve you, your love, your patience, or your forgiveness. I love you."

"Why?" The words are quiet, but the request roars in my subconscious.

"Why?" He sits back and looks me in the eye. "Because you are you, Sophie, I can't explain why, I just do. When I saw you, this beautiful girl so unaware of herself, so real, I was struck. And when I looked into those big green eyes and you batted your long lashes at me, I forgot to breathe, everything changed. When I touched you it was like magic, and then you made me waffles." He grins. "I love waffles."

"My whole life I have been surrounded by blindingly shiny objects, Sophie. Beautiful on the outside, but dull and mass produced at heart. I was always chasing the bigger, better model, each one more shiny and superficial than the last. I was in a mindless, pointless competition with myself. I realize now that the real commodity lies in the rare gem, unique, unlike any other, and irreplaceable, something that I alone possess. You are that rare gem. I want your heart, Sophie, I want all of you. It's only fair, you already have all of me."

I shift in the small bed, careful not to tug on his IV or the web of tubes and wires that keep him plugged into the nurses' station. I straddle his lap and he runs his hands up my back and under my shirt. His hands are cold, but soft and gentle. His fingers traverse the length of my back and he pushes my shirt up over my hips.

"We won't be needing this," he teases, pulling it up over my breasts.

"Rhys," I feign protest, stopping him momentarily from pulling my shirt over my head. "The nurse."

"She won't be back for hours Sophie, we're alone, baby. Please, let me feel you. I've missed you." I relent easily and quickly forget my worries as he slips his fingers beneath my breasts and pops them up and out of my bra, standing at attention and eye level as they spill over the cup. His eyes grow in hunger, and he grips my flesh with purpose. I feel him grow beneath me and my hips roll against him of their own accord. I lean down to kiss him and he moans before giving me his lips, his tongue taking the lead.

He licks my lips before pulling me into his mouth, our tongues dancing. We kiss until I am out of breath, until the room spins and I completely forget where I am. I press myself into his hands while he kneads my breasts before he pulls one into his mouth, covering as much of my flesh he can before sucking me in. The pull of his mouth sends me reeling and I grip his hair and give him more. He bites me, leaving my nipple red and tight before moving to the other side.

The way he covers me with his mouth is heavenly, every nerve ending awakening and vibrating from his breath, his power, his hunger. He wraps his arm around the small of my back and pulls me closer, his eyes focused on mine as he sucks and bites at my tits. I throw my head back as he bites me again, his hands holding me steady in his lap.

"Mr. Slate!" Ripped from the moment, I turn to see the nurse standing at the door with an embarrassed, impressed grin across her puckered little face. Mortified, I try to cover myself as she slides the door closed behind her and steps into the middle of the room, not even pretending to avert her eyes. "Well, you seem to have quickly regained your vigor," she winks, "but, may I remind you that you are hooked up to a heart monitor, and any spike in your blood pressure will bring one of us running." She checks the heart monitor before tapping a few buttons, and then turns to me as I gingerly climb off the bed with my shirt held in front of me. "As we are glad that Mr. Slate is feeling…. able, we recommend that you wait at least until he is discharged." My face must be on fire, I can feel the red in my cheeks as she turns back to him. "Dr. Holder will see you in the morning. I'd venture to say the chances of you being discharged are good. But until then I must insist that you get some rest."

Dr. Holder shows up first thing in the morning with a knowing twinkle in his eye as he grins and shakes my hand.

"I understand you are eager to be discharged Mr. Slate. And as I am aware of your renewed strength it is the nature of the swelling in your brain that has me concerned. I would like to keep you for at least another forty-eight hours to ensure that swelling has completely subsided, and we will want to do an x-ray on that hip. Just be patient and we will have you out of here as quickly as possible. I just signed the papers for your father. He will be going home this evening."

His swelling continues to go down and the x-rays show a hairline fracture but nothing too serious on his hip. The angry scar on his flesh is the worst of that injury. Three more days of nosey nurses and restless sleep at his side until he finally receives his walking papers.

Matthew and Olivia are waiting for us when we arrive home. Matthew tries to help Rhys up the stairs, but he refuses, being stubborn as ever. He follows him upstairs while Olivia and I flit around the kitchen out of habit. Nothing has changed; it is just as I left it all, with the addition of three empty bottles of scotch on the counter, tangible evidence of his confessed desperation.

"So, did you talk to him?" I turn to answer her, and we are nose to nose. I take a step back and reflect her stance, hand on my hip, head cocked to the side.

"Yes, we talked, obviously. He brought it up first thing." We have a stare off before I crack and laugh at her. "He spilled his guts and I let him."

"Good," she returns quickly, "I know that Nadja has caused all of this, but he had a hand in creating it. He needs to take responsibility and treat you right, Sophie, I swear." She tears a piece of bread and pops it into her mouth.

"You realize that you just ate a carb, right?" I tease moving around her.

"I don't even care anymore," she mumbles, her mouth full of bread. "I am just hungry all the time."

"Eating for two?" I tease, but she finds no humor in it, snapping back at me.

"No!" I just look at her, searching for a crack in her facade. "I mean, his mother would die of happiness, but I'm just not sure I'm ready for that."

"Well, are you being safe?"

"Not exactly. Matthew says he is ready, I am just hoping that my body is listening to me."

"Olivia!" I laugh, "Sweetie, we both know that is not how it works."

"Oh, hush, Sophie, I'm dealing with this the best

way I know how. I can't think about it, it's too much to consider. I can't believe people make these decisions on purpose. I'd rather just leave it to chance. If it happens, it happens. We will deal with it then, but now, back to Rhys."

"Olivia the man is lying in bed, just home from the hospital. Can't we give him a break?"

"A small break, but, Sophie, you have to stick up for yourself. You can't let that bitch push you around and you can't allow him to hide things from you anymore. You deserve better, damn it." I kiss her swiftly on the cheek as I pass; grateful I have her looking out for me.

Matthew appears an hour or so later as we sip our first glass of wine. His face lights up when he lays eyes on Olivia and his ardor is contagious. As he looks at her, the love he feels for her shines through his eyes, yet she seems totally unfazed. I'd give my right arm for someone to look at me like that. I wonder if Rhys looks at me that way and I just don't notice. *Nah*.

Olivia doesn't even finish her wine. Within moments, he sweeps her out the door and off to dinner. I make my way upstairs to check on Rhys.

CH. 8

I find him propped up in his oversized bed, pillows surrounding him, a laptop already opened, his phone waiting on the nightstand. I shake my head, wanting him to rest, but I know that he won't. He watches me as I cross the room

"Is there anything I can get for you?" I ask, hopping onto the end of the bed.

"What I really want is scotch and a cigar, Beautiful."

"You are not supposed to have either, Rhys, and you were there when the doctor said as much."

"I just thought that, perhaps, since you love me," he winks, "maybe you would bend the rules for me." His sly grin and twinkling eyes make me weak. "Please," he mouths, flashing that damn dimple and looking positively helpless. I sigh in resignation, not even putting up a fight, wanting too badly to see that coy smile on his face. When I return to the room, his eyes are closed and his mouth slack. I put the scotch on the bedside table and crawl in next to him, but as I do, I see the smile rise on his face and he pulls me close with a growl in his throat.

"Mmmmm, I miss the feel of you, Beautiful, the smell of your hair, the taste of your skin," he mumbles against my neck, his lips sweeping across my delicate skin like a paintbrush. "I love you, Sophie. I'm never going to let you go again." And as I open my eyes, he is staring straight through me, consuming my soul with the fire in his eyes, and I know that I will never leave this man. My heart would crumble to dust and I would cease to exist as one surely cannot survive without their heart, and he certainly owns mine. Lock and key. He winces as he reaches for the scotch, and I sit up to help.

"No, Beautiful, I can get it," he groans as he sits slowly upright and adjusts himself against the bank of pillows at his back. "I don't want you waiting on me," he says as he swirls the scotch in his glass, watching the amber liquid dash up the sides only to slide back down in a delicious, aromatic dance. Before he takes his sip, he offers me the glass, tipping it to my lips. I take a shallow sip, pulling the essence of the scotch into my nose, the essence of Rhys. He takes his drink and rests the glass in his lap.

I snip the tip of his cigar and hand it to him, offering him a light. He puffs and puffs until he is eclipsed by a cloud of smoke and I toss the lighter on the table. He settles in and I fit nicely into his side, the missing piece to his puzzle. We sit in silence while he puffs away, watching smoke rings meander across the room as our hearts reconnect and settle into a perfect rhythm. I take the cigar from his fingers and pull a few shallow hits before gingerly climbing over him and placing it in the ashtray. He pulls me into his lap and I straddle him, careful not to put any weight on him, afraid to hurt him.

"I'm not so frail, Sophie. I want to feel the weight of you, please, Beautiful, don't be afraid. You won't hurt me." His fingers dig into my hips as he pulls me down from my knees, coaxing me into his lap. I relent, but still hover as he places his hand over my heart, his fingers digging ever so slightly into my flesh. "This is mine," he says, silently signing his deed of ownership over my heart.

Melting over him slowly, I press against him as his cock grows beneath me. His hands fist in my hair and he steadies my face, "I need to feel you, Sophie. All of you. I need to feel that pussy quiver as I sink into you. I want you to take me hostage and never let me go." His breathing increases and becomes shallower with each passing word, and his eyes darken like those of a hunting wolf zeroing in on his prey. He looks as if he could devour me and I want him to, every last inch of flesh, every single drop of blood. I need him to consume me before the fire within does.

He pulls my face to him and swallows me with a kiss that could ignite the world. His mouth moves against mine as his tongue invades a willing territory. Biting my lips as I suckle his tongue, he kisses me so deep that I forget to breathe and I dive headfirst into the abyss, wanting to be carried away by his heavenly mouth, the tide of his tongue, the force of his love, and the heat of his lust. When he finally pulls back, I'm so lost for breath I'm dizzy and half out of my mind.

"Show me, Sophie; show me what I've been dreaming about, what I saw in my mind's eye, what I want, what I need, and what is mine." I climb from the bed and stand before him, ready, more than ready, desperate. And in an instant, under his gaze, everything falls away. He strips me with his eyes before I ever strip away a stitch of clothing, and I know I have nothing to fear. This man loves me. I pull my shirt slowly over my head, stretching my arms high above me, exposing my soft belly, my hips swaying as I pull the shirt from my arms and surrender it to the floor. The corner of his mouth curls in that damn crooked grin and I start to rush, tugging at my jeans and the fucking button.

"Slow down, Beautiful, we have all night," he chuckles, sitting up against the pillows. "I want every moment to last a lifetime, my love." I melt where I stand as his words sink into my bones. *My love*. Nothing has ever felt so good, my heart swells, my pussy drips, and a singular, ecstatic tear rolls down my cheek as I hook my thumbs into my jeans and slide them down my legs, careful to run my fingers along my thighs, igniting little fires that I'm sure he will stoke. I step from my jeans leaving them in a pool of dark denim at my feet and stand before him in just my panties and bra. Nothing fancy, just me in all my ordinary glory, pink cotton panties and a basic T-shirt bra, but the way he looks upon me makes me feel like I'm dripping in diamonds and dipped in gold, the most precious of treasures.

"My God, you are beautiful," he whispers with such admiration in his eyes that I couldn't possibly doubt him. I reach behind me and unhook my bra, letting the straps fall from my shoulders, dropping it to the floor before me. The cool air caresses my skin and my nipples stand at attention, eager for his brand of lust. He is watchful, appreciative of every soft inch. I lick my lips and muster the tiniest bit of courage as I slip my panties down my legs and stand before him, completely naked, completely his. He rakes me over with his deep green eyes, traveling over each dip and curve, reading me like a book, and I just stand there happy to let him see me dripping with anticipation and a confidence I have never known. In all my naked glory, I am happy to stand before him, proud to belong to him, and eager to show him how amazing he has made me feel.

"Come here," he commands and I go to his side without a second thought. He places his hand on my tummy and I flinch, only slightly, but he isn't having any of it. "Don't," he says sternly, his finger beneath my chin, tipping my head to force me to look him in the eyes. "Don't ever shrink from my touch, Sophie; don't ever try to hide what is mine. I love you, worship you, every fucking inch. Do you understand?" I nod slightly, but it's not good enough. "I said, do you understand?"

"Yes, I understand." He wraps his hand around my waist and pulls me to the edge of the bed. "Don't ever doubt how beautiful you are, Sophie, never again. Now," he pauses as he shifts his legs, "climb onto my lap, Beautiful."

I climb into his lap, straddling him, careful not to put too much weight on him, but he won't be treated with kid gloves. He pulls me down and I settle with his clothed cock between my legs. Releasing a deep sigh, he runs his fingers along my collarbone, sending a tremor down my spine, followed by his soft lips, dragging them across my neck, igniting every inch of skin. Our mouths dance slowly at first; biting and suckling at one another until he takes me with his full force, stealing my breath in the same moment. His hands slide down my sides resting for a moment on my hips, his fingers exploring and recording every soft dimple and curve of my body. His eyes shine with a carnal lust that makes me so wet I could be drowning, and here I sit, atop my man. A man that loves me; there is nowhere else I would rather be.

He watches my eyes as he slips a finger between my lips, exploring the warm depths he so inflames and without warning, he plunges into me, first one finger, then two. His eyes flare with purpose as I gasp and adjust to his welcomed assault. Pumping his fingers into me, he pushes me up from his lap creating a daunting rhythm that makes my thighs burn. His other hand moves to my chest and he grips my breast in his massive fist. Bringing my flesh to his mouth, he bites down hard on my nipple, pulling it through his teeth as he watches my eyes grow in delight and in pain. He moves from one breast to the other, torturing, biting, and sucking on my skin until I'm marked by his sinful mouth. I watch the bruises bloom under my skin and revel in the feeling of the blood rushing back. He kisses the base of my throat as he slips his hand around the back of my neck, holding me steady, forcing me to watch him as his nostrils flare and his concentration focuses. He works my body like a tool, a tool he is at once familiar with and still eager to learn. I sink onto his fingers, pulling him into me and grind against his palm, needy and wanting more, but he just chuckles.

"Oh no, Beautiful," he shakes his head playfully, his eyes hooded and dark. "We aren't going there yet, I want you to beg. I want you to be as desperate as I am."

"But, I am," I moan, tilting my head back, wanting everything.

"No, I don't think you are," he smirks as he slides yet another finger into my pussy, stretching me wide, pumping into me like a drill. Just as he begins to hit a spot that makes me want to scream, his thumb presses to my clit and I jerk in his lap. "Oh, a little sensitive are we?" he asks with a wink, making a meal out of torturing me. Sweet, delightful torture. His grip tightens on my neck as he plunges his fingers into me over and over, curled around so he hits that soft spot that drives me wild, that spot that only he knows, that he discovered. I buck and ride his hand until he is soaked and I'm winded and I can't wait another minute.

"Please," I mewl in a labored whisper.

"Please what, my love?" I look into his wicked eyes and cannot control my mouth for another second. Every ounce of inhibition goes out the window as he thrust his fingers up into me, and I scream, "Please Rhys, I need your cock. I need to feel you, all of you. Please for God's sake, fuck me now!" I'm shaking my head side to side positively possessed with the thought of his cock. I need it now.

"That's what I wanted, Beautiful." he exclaims, pulling his fingers from my pussy and freeing his cock in one fell swoop. Without a moment's hesitation, I wind my fist around his pulsing cock and watch him slip his fingers into his mouth, his sleepy eyes lighting up as he moans and licks each finger clean. A ferocious lust grows behind his eyes and he grabs me by the hips and guides me over him, sliding into me at a fool's pace; inch by inch he controls me as I sink and try to swallow him. Stretching me open and claiming what is his, I have never wanted to be owned, to be possessed as fully as I do in this moment. I want him to take me over completely, and in his eyes I see his glee as he reads me like a book.

"Yes, Beautiful, I see it in your eyes. Do it my love, just let go; I will always take care of you." As the last words fall from his beautiful mouth, he slams into me, his whole pulsing length possessing me and I am found. Never have I felt so whole, so complete, and so full. He takes me by the hips and sets his pace, steady and measured. Each thrust deliberate and brutal until he hits a spot that makes my blood sing. Like a chorus on high, each and every time his cock hits that spot, I am less and less in control of my body. Nailing it now dead on, so deep, and so wild, my hair thrashes about my face as I try to keep pace, try to ride him like a fucking bull, and then he stops. So deep within me, pressing against that sweet spot, he stops and watches my eyes burn. He holds me still, won't let me move, as a hunger grows so rabid in me that I may just go fucking insane.

Slowly again he starts to move, holding me still, fucking into me like a jackhammer. Faster and faster he begins to pummel me, each time hitting that spot. Like an itch I cannot scratch, so deep. Every time he thrusts against it, I growl at him, fucking needy, wanting more, needing more. It's an addiction to feel him deep within me, stroking that tiny spot that belongs fully to him. Each time more intense than the last until my eyes roll back and I hear him whisper, "Let go, Sophie."

One last brutal thrust and I tighten my strangle hold on him before I explode, my pussy pulses and gushes, soaking him, soaking us both. My body begins to shake, my legs trembling, my hands grip his shoulders and I hold on for dear life and ride it out. Feeling like I'm being ripped apart, good Lord in heaven, I couldn't stop shaking if I wanted. As I come down, he thrusts up into me again and again, forcing me to come over and over, until tears streak down my face, his fingers surely tattooed upon my skin now as his grip is brutal and deliberate. When he finally empties himself, I feel his heat invade my body, a lovely white hot heat that fills me utterly. With his neck craned to the ceiling, his eyes focused solely on me, and his body, his broken and battered body beneath me, I immediately come back into myself and try to lift up from his lap, but he refuses.

"No, Beautiful, I need to feel you. I will not let you go," he mutters against the sweat slicked skin of my throat before running his tongue to the base of my ear. He takes my lobe between his teeth and pulls before his warm lips rest against my ear. "You are my everything, Sophie. I just want to stay connected like this for as long as possible. Please don't go"

"I'm not going anywhere, Rhys. I just don't want to hurt you."

"You could never hurt me, Beautiful, never."

CH. 9

The next few days passed without any complication. Rhys rested and I doted. It was nice, comfortable, and I felt useful and needed. The third morning we woke with the sun and made slow love with the windows open while the birds came alive with the day. I was able to get him up and out for a leisurely walk around the block only to return to the most unpleasant company; a stretch limo, blackened windows, the driver standing sentry. As we approach the car, the door opens and out steps Bianca, just as one would expect her to be, draped in Chanel and a strand of pearls. Her hair perfectly coiffed, make-up flawless, but her practiced smile falls from her face the moment our eyes meet, a crack in her well cultivated shell.

"Mother," I try to retreat behind him, but he squeezes my hand and pulls me closer. She hesitates, then steps closer to place a cool kiss on his cheek, careful not to come near me. "Now is really not a good time. We just took a walk and I'm a bit worse for wear."

"Well, I'll just come in for a moment and help you get comfortable and make sure you are taken care of. I brought you some groceries." She starts up the steps motioning for her driver, who holds a grocery bag and cake box, to follow her.

"No, Mother, now is not a good time." She stops and looks at him; confusion, irritation and embarrassment creeping from her eyes.

"Rhys."

"Bianca," he doesn't miss a beat. Pulling me up the stairs past her, he swings me towards the door and turns to grab the grocery bag and cake box. "Sophie is taking very good care of me. I will let you know when I am ready to receive company, Mother. Thank you for the gifts." He lifts them in the air and steps through the door, handing them to me. He turns to close the door on her stunned face. "Goodbye, Mother."

Glee, disbelief and exasperation mix in his eyes when he turns to me. He pulls me to him, brushing his lips across mine before claiming my mouth. I taste the desperation, the urgency in the thrust of his tongue. When he finally lets me go, my bottom lip is swelling from his bite and I am breathless.

"I want to take you away, somewhere where I can relax and recuperate and we can be together in peace. Say yes." I follow him into the living room; he pats his lap, inviting me in as he settles on the couch. I straddle him and wrap my arms around his neck.

"Yes." I kiss him slowly as he wraps his hands around me, gripping my hips, pulling me closer.

"That was easy." His warm breath tickles my ear.

"I think you'll find that I can be very easy, Mr. Slate." I tease, nipping at his lip, but not letting him consume my mouth. I turn my head and direct him to my neck. "That was not a very nice way to treat your mother," I whisper as he covers my collarbone with his warm lips.

"She deserved it." he mumbles as he continues to coat my neck with kisses. "After the way she treated you, she is lucky I am talking to her at all." A small smile of triumph twists my mouth as he pulls my ear between his teeth and he quietly roars, "I love you, Sophie Rose, I want you to understand how much. There was nothing before you, and there will be nothing after." The growing lump in my throat makes it hard to breathe while his fingers wind in my hair. "You wiped it all away. There can only be you. You are the only woman in the world as far as I am concerned, my saving grace, and my home." I take his face between my hands, his eyes shining with sincerity and lust while my eyes are clouded by love.

"I didn't know I was lonely before I met you. I have been reaching for things, collecting…. women. I had my head buried in the sand, blinded by my goals, driven by the greed around me. And all the while, all I really needed was you. You are my prize." He shakes his head at me, looking so exasperated. "I wish I could just…tie you down and make you understand."

"Why do you need to tie me down to make me understand?" I shift in his lap, resting my head on his shoulder. "Have *you* ever been restrained?"

"No," he laughs. "I like to be in charge, Sophie."

"That doesn't seem fair."

"Do you want to tie me up, Sophie?" He looks at me with a quiet determination while I contemplate the notion of being in control. His body tied down and at my mercy, touching him at will, anywhere I want. *Yes, please!* But, I play coy and resolve to form a plan, to keep that notion in my back pocket.

"Maybe, I do." The wolfish grin comes out and his eyes sparkle in anticipation. "But, not now."

"What is wrong with now?" There's a challenge in his look and I know the thought makes him excited as well.

"I think the lesson would be lost."

"So you want to teach me a lesson?" He shifts me from his lap and stands, towering above me, looking down into my eyes with an unmistakable hunger.

"Perhaps," I return, coquettishly, "I think there are a few things you could stand to learn. You should know how it feels, however, it seems rather unfair when you are so frail and helpless," I tease.

"Frail and helpless?" he snorts, indignant with a slight chuckle, "Well, I will look forward to my upcoming lesson, and showing you just how frail I am." That crooked grin makes an appearance and almost sets me aflame.

He heads into his office and begins with the travel arrangements right away; sending me to Olivia's to get my bags, refusing to tell me where we are going. The only hint is to bring my passport.

Olivia is beside herself with glee, flitting around my room, offering me various pieces of her wardrobe. She brings dresses and heels, bags and necklaces.

"Liv, I really doubt I will need any of that. He said we were going to find peace and recuperate. We aren't going on vacation."

"I thought you didn't know where you were going?" She slips a little black dress into my luggage.

"I don't, but I don't want to over pack."

"Just one casual dress, then, I promise. But, you never know Sophie, it's better to be over prepared than under prepared."

"Ok, Liv, one dress. Thank you."

Olivia and Matthew drive me back to Rhys'. Olivia walks me in while Matthew moves my bags from his trunk to Rhys 'car. Olivia wastes no time embarrassing me as she asks Rhys where we are going and why almost the moment we hit the door.

"I need to know where you are taking my girl, Rhys. It will put me at ease knowing she is properly prepared. So, where are you heading?" He looks to me with an infectious, truly happy smile.

"Home." His smile brightens, as does Olivia's. "I am taking Sophie home with me. We are going to Tulla for a few weeks, going to visit my family, where the world cannot get to us." My heart leaps into my throat and I am elated and terrified! I have always wanted to go to Ireland, and I desperately want to know Rhys' family, but, Ireland? I've never left the country.

CH. 10

We collect our bags and cross the parking lot to a sleek, silver Mercedes. Dropping our bags behind the trunk, I look to Rhys and he is eyeballing Charlie who wears a mischievous smirk.

"Ay, Cousin, I do believe I am off the clock ye see. I'm confident you can hoist your own bags into the boot, and don't forget the lady's bags as well." He winks and tips his hat before walking around the car and climbing into the back seat.

I watch Rhys adjust the mirrors and his seat, buckle his seat belt and start the car all the while watching Charlie through the rear view. Charlie merely grins.

"Now, if ye don't mind, I'll catch a bit of rest on the way home, driver." He taps Rhys' seat and sits back, pulling his cap down over his face barely hiding the wide smile he boasts. Rhys presses down on the gas and before I know it, we are winding through the greenest countryside I have ever seen. Rolling emerald hills, craggy outcroppings and thatched roof cottages pepper the landscape.

"This is Tulla." We slow to a crawl as we skirt the village center and out of town we go. "This is where I grew up."

"But…" I turn and look out the back window watching his childhood disappear behind us.

"Don't worry, we will go into town one day, I'm just impatient to get home," and as he says it, I feel the sincerity in his voice, the pull he has to this place. This really is his home, his family. Over rolling hills and down through narrow roads cut through the peat, we roam for what feels like not long enough before he pulls down a tree lined lane. The willows shake hands across the road, bowing and swaying as we drive through the lovely shaded tunnel they create. When the sun breaks through again and we leave the trees behind, a wide open swath of the most beautiful countryside opens up and at the bottom of the hill we are perched upon sits a gray stone house.

I don't know what I was expecting, but a stone cottage was not it. I felt myself sink a bit. Perhaps in the back of my romance addled mind, I expected a proper Irish manor, a country house. I've watched too much Downton Abbey. This is not what I would expect from the Slate family. This looks like original roots, this is heaven, and this is the real Rhys.

"There she is," he sighs, "home." Down the hill, and the sun seems to follow us as if to welcome Rhys home herself. Chickens bustle about a feed yard that sits to the left of the house enclosed by a low stone fence. There is a small herd of sheep I can barely make out meandering down the field behind the house, but as we come down the hill I lose sight of them. The blue sky meeting the jewel green turf is overwhelming and my heart swells. And I swear I can hear a fiddle in my head as we pull around a half moon drive and up in front of this tall, stone house surrounded by a high stone wall with a bright red front gate. Rhys turns to me and lights up the car with the most gleeful grin I have ever seen before the gate flies open and a mob of young men push their way out the too narrow passageway.

"Aye, Rhys!" One shouts as he pushes two others out of his way with his broad shoulders, effectively blocking the door to get first rights. I look over at Charlie, still snoring, fast asleep and completely unaware until the back door is yanked open by one of the other men and they slap him across the head with his cap.

"Wake up ye fool, Mother's missing her precious bairn! Oh," he stops as our eyes meet and he smirks with a familiar twist of his mouth, "well, hello, lass." He reaches across Charlie and offers his hand, I offer my hand back and he pulls me towards him with a Cheshire grin and kisses my hand never looking away from my eyes. "Are ye Charlie's girl then? You know I'm the better brother, lass."

"Aye!" Charlie snaps as he sits up and breaks our handshake. "The better brother indeed. The lady hasn't even left the car and look at ye! Already hounding her like a rabid mutt. Back up, William, would ye and give Sophie some room."

"Sophie," he says, slowly in his broguish tongue, "a beautiful name fer a beautiful lass." He winks and backs out of the car letting Charlie stand up. Rhys opens my door and extends a hand to me helping me from the car, saving me from William.

"Aye, William, this here is Sophie and she's *mine*, and I'll thank you to keep your dirty paws off her." The roll of his tongue sets me on fire and I watch him for a split second in awe before he takes me in the most passionate, theatrical kiss for all to see. The men break out in cheers and slap one another on the back as they funnel us through the gate with a roar of laughter. In the courtyard there are two huge Irish wolfhounds lounging in the shade of a large weeping willow and a few stray chickens that seem to have escaped their enclosure. A large double door to the right is propped open to reveal a sprawling country kitchen.

I listen to the men welcome Rhys home and try to get a feel for who everyone is. There is a kinship here I've missed so sorely in my own life. A consuming love for one another that is at once overwhelming and completely comforting. Rhys turns and pulls me in front of him, whistling to catch the attention of the small crowd.

"Aye, cousins, this is Sophie, Ms. Noelle, if you know your manners." He winks at me before kissing me on the cheek. "You treat her like family and you'll not catch the wrath of me!" He points into the crowd and starts shouting names, as if I will ever remember. "William and Finn, that over there's Patrick, you know Charlie." They jeer him, hoot and holler in silly protest before they are broken up by the appearance of a most angelic creature. Long, dark, strawberry blond hair pours over her shoulder in a plump braid. Her pale green eyes sparkle from twenty-five yards away. She is tall and slender.

"I'd like to see that, I would." She stops and rakes me over for a moment and winks at me before turning her gleaming smile to him.

"There she is, the emerald in the Slate family crown! Colleen, bring yourself over here and give me a hug." She is quite possibly one of the most beautiful young women I have seen in my life. Her pale peach skin appears translucent in the late day sun, a swath of light brown freckles dot the bridge of her nose, and those Slate family eyes that would set her apart from anyone. She is a true beauty, a beauty among beasts it would seem.

"My goodness, little Colleen, every time I see you, you get more beautiful. Thank God, you are tucked away here in the country.

"Aye, Cousin, when will you let me come see ye in New York?"

"Oh," he shakes his head with a grin, "uh-uh, not any time soon!" She hits him playfully on the arm and pulls away from him turning her attentions to me.

"He is such a right brute!" she proclaims,

before embracing me and whispering in my ear, "Welcome, Sophie, lovely to know ya." She pulls away from me and grabs my hand. "Come now, let's leave the animals be, Mam'll be wanting to meet ye. It's not every day Rhys brings home a girl, not ever in fact!" She giggles as she pulls me through the large kitchen door and away from Rhys.

"Mam, we've got a visitor," Colleen calls as we step into the large kitchen. A long farmhouse table sits in the middle of the room piled high with potatoes and greens. The floor is rough and uneven lending and an old air to the room. The walls are covered in bright white plaster with arched door frames and windows. The far wall is dominated by a large archway that looks like it may once have been a hearth, but now houses a large stove. I look around and fall in love with every inch of the space, the old and new mixed in to a cobbling of memories and meals.

"So, what have we here then?" She wipes her hands on the apron that hangs around her hips as she emerges from what I assume is the butler's pantry; short, shorter than Colleen at least, a beaming jovial smile on her face and a bright blush across her cheeks. She wears the freckles of an Irish woman with an angelic grace, her strawberry hair, peppered with gray, sits atop of her head in a full bun, a falling tendril tickling at her nose. She wipes it away with the back of her hand and steps closer to me, as if to inspect me.

"Yer the girl, are ya?" Her face takes a stern set and I'm nervous, wanting her to approve of me.

"Yes, Ma'am," I manage, more meager than I had intended. "I'm Sophie." I extend my hand to her, but she just looks at it.

"So, ye are." Standing stock still for a split second, she knocks the wind out of me with a cold breeze before sweeping me into her arms like a joyful mother. "It's lovely to meet ye, Sophie, welcome to our home," she says as she pinches my face then pats my now red cheeks. "Colleen, fetch her an apron." She smiles at me and points me towards the table. "I'll be needing your help if we are to feed these boys tonight, Sophie. Can ye peel a potato?"

Colleen hands me a patchwork apron and a paring knife. "Yes, Ma'am," I reply as I slip the apron over my head.

***

We sit down to dinner at a long table that the men have assembled in the courtyard. Colleen sets the table with jugs of water and two large casks of what I assume is beer. The boys file out of the kitchen, each with a dish in their hands. Roasted pig, steaming vegetables, boiled potatoes, greens, a board of fresh cheeses, and loaves of Irish bread with freshly churned butter that smells like heaven. As everyone settles in, Brigid takes her seat at the head of the table and Rhys takes his seat next to me. The food circles the table as everyone helps themselves. A well-rehearsed silence befalls the feast the moment everyone's plates are full. Hands in their laps, they all bow their heads as Colleen says a prayer over the meal.

"Bless, O Lord, this food we are about to eat; and we pray, You, O God, that it may be good for our body and soul; and if there be any poor creature hungry or thirsty walking along the road, send them into us that we can share the food with them, just as You share your gifts with all of us. And thank ye, Lord, for returning my brother and Rhys safely to us and for bringing Sophie into our home."

Slainte! They all call in unison before raising their glasses.

"Halt!" William calls as he pushes himself away from the table. "Hold yer glasses," he grumbles as he walks into the kitchen, returning with a burlap sleeve. "I do believe this calls for a special toast. I just happen to have the perfect thing." He pulls a bottle from the burlap and sets it down in front of Rhys. "Aye, what do you think, Cousin?" Rhys lifts the crystal bottle and turns it in his hands with a grin.

"Is this what I think it is?" he asks, lifting the bottle to the fading sunlight, watching the light play off the dark amber liquid.

"Aye, our first bottle, just in time for your arrival. Been aged for four long years."

"Shall we have a taste then?" He grins at me with his eyebrow perched high on his forehead before handing the bottle back to William to pour. Two fingers in a dozen juice glasses and the bottle is no longer.

"Now, for a proper toast," William says as he raises his glass to Rhys. Rhys pushes back from the table and stands, his glass stretched high above the table.

"Here's to women's kisses, and to whiskey, amber clear; Not as sweet as a woman's kiss, but a darn sight more sincere!"

He winks at me before they roar *Slainte!* again, and I follow suit as they all take a deep sip of their whiskey and dig into their plates of hot food.

CH. 11

The call of the rooster wakes us both as we cling to each other in the small wrought iron double bed. Rhys pulls me to his side and I mold to his form, snuggling into his neck, the very best smell first thing in the morning. My body immediately springs to life and I kiss his warm flesh, making my way towards his ear, when his phone rings and I've lost him. I hop out of bed and pull on a pair of shorts as he rolls over for his phone. As soon as he sees the number, his face twists in a most unhappy mask and I quickly excuse myself.

"I'll go make us some tea."

"Ok, my love, this shouldn't take long," he says with his hand over the phone, waiting for me to leave the room.

The house is quiet and the sun not fully risen in the sky. Barefoot, I slink down the stairs, through the sitting room and into the kitchen where I find Brigid.

"I'm sorry, I didn't mean to disturb you."

"Oh no, child, I am just enjoying the first moments of the day, it's peaceful, won't stay this way for long. Join me," she says, reaching for a second tea cup. "So, how did ye meet our Rhys?"

"His best friend Matthew is married to my best friend. We met first at their wedding." I run my finger around the rim of the delicate china tea cup, slightly nervous, but wanting to know her, wanting her to know me.

"And ye have been together ever since then?" she questions, fetching a pint of cream from the fridge.

"Not exactly," I reply with a grin.

"No, nothing is that easy, is it? Of course, the harder we have to work for something, the more value it holds in our hearts, wouldn't you agree?" She looks at me as if waiting for the answers to the very questions of the universe.

"Yes, Ma'am," is all I can come up with.

"Tell me about your family, then, Sophie."

"My parents have passed," I tell her, gazing down into my almost empty cup, "and I've just recently lost my grandmother, so I suppose," I pause to take the last sip of my tea, "I don't have a family anymore." Looking up into her eyes, I am already regretting such a somber statement, but the light reflected is not one of pity, but of love and concern.

"Family is where the love lies, ma' dear, I dare say that my Rhys is your new family," she winks and finishes her tea, and I just watch, dumbfounded and speechless. "Ye seem like a good girl, Sophie. He needs someone true in his life, he deserves that. I love him like he's my own. Come now, help me round up some breakfast." She pushes away from the table and slips on a pair of well-worn wellies that wait by the back door and motions to another pair that I step into.

She hands me a large woven basket and I follow her across a wide green field boxed in by a beautifully craggy, old stone fence and through a little wooden gate. A small but prolific garden hides behind the mossy stones. She picks plump, ripe tomatoes just warm from the rising morning sun and digs handfuls of potatoes from a small plot, dropping it all in my basket.

"It's good for him to be here, he belongs here," she muses as we cross the field to another stone enclosure. This one opens to the field and is populated with colorful hens, pecking and clucking their morning greeting. She wades through the hens to the small wooden hen house and begins pulling eggs from a little door, using her apron as a sling. "Well, bring yourself over here, ma' dear, don't need to be dropping these eggs before their kin."

We return to the house, and she begins washing potatoes.

"Can I help?" I ask, watching her go through the motions as if she is programmed. She has probably done this same ritual every morning for untold years, thus the rhythm of this house, the comfortable rhythm of the whole country as I've experienced so far.

"Aye, it'd be my pleasure and is in fact my duty, ma' dear, to teach you how to make my Rhys a proper Irish breakfast. If he is to love you, you must know how to feed him." She chuckles and bumps me with her hip, sweeping by me to pull a side of Irish bacon from the refrigerator.

Colleen appears fresh faced and ready for the day and gets right to work on cracking the eggs. The boys filter into the kitchen and take their seats around the table, pouring orange juice and tea, talking about the days to come. When Rhys finally makes his appearance, it is clear his mood is dark. His eyes are hooded, his mouth turned down and when he smiles at me it doesn't meet his eyes. I take my seat next to him as breakfast begins. The table is buzzing with talk of the upcoming days, the places Rhys must take me and the people he must see while we are here. He listens and answers, but I can see his heart is not here; he is distracted.

"What's wrong?" I whisper in his ear, but he brushes me off with a shrug and a wink, turning to William to discuss a visit to somewhere, but they don't say where. A few times from across the table I catch Brigid watching me, she always offers a smile or a wink as if to encourage me. When breakfast is finished, they all abandon the table and disappear into the courtyard, leaving Colleen and me to clean up. We clear the dishes while Brigid sits and finishes her tea.

"Rhys seems out of sorts this morning." She looks to me in question, but I have no answer. The only thing I can guess is the phone call.

"I'm sure it's probably just work," I shrug and finish drying the dishes that Colleen hands me. I walk out into the courtyard and find him sitting under a tree, his phone in one hand, his head in the other.

"What's got you so grouchy this morning?" I sit next to him and he puts his arm around my shoulder and forces a smile.

"Nothing for you to worry about," he grins, but it's not real. "Now, why don't you go run and shower. We're going out for a couple of hours."

"Are you sure you are up for it?" I don't want him to wear himself out; after all, we are here so he can recover. But I'm elated at the idea of being able to take in some of the country and being with him in his element.

"Yes, Sophie, I'm fine. Don't worry, now go," he urges me away as he focuses again on his phone.

I emerge from the shower to find our room empty. I pull on a pair of jeans and a T-shirt and head downstairs to find Rhys brooding at the kitchen table; his laptop fired up, his furious fingers flying across the keys. He looks up at me like a man possessed, yet, in an instant, I watch him slip his mask on. The emotion leaves his face replaced with that practiced smile and dull, unconvincing light behind his eyes.

"Are you ready for a scenic drive this morning, Sophie? It's time to check on the investments."

"Oh yes!" I can't hold back my excitement. I have always wanted to travel, always wanted to explore, and now I have my Rhys as a guide? What could be better? Perhaps his mood, but I'm sure we can solve that. Whatever it is, we will squash it and I will soak up every moment like the last rays of the sun. A small smile breaks his mask and I know his mood can, and will, turn. "But, you shouldn't be working."

"This isn't work, Sophie, this is family."

We drive through the countryside, floating over emerald hills dotted with sheep. The land is cut into swaths, defined by old rock walls that look as if they could fall at any moment, yet appear to have been standing for centuries. We coast along the River Shannon and watch as narrow estuaries become so wide we lose sight of the opposite bank. Ruins blend into the landscape; the hard gray shell of a life gone by seems to be perched atop every hill. We turn away from the river and head north into a barren landscape. Barren outcroppings and ancient Dolmens guard the alien land and a great rocky expanse stretches out before us.

"This is the Burren, ever heard of it?" he asks. As we slow, he points to an outcropping a few yards ahead. A massive slab of granite is precariously perched atop two narrow legs. "They say they are the graves of giants. Around here, we were always taught they were portals, but to where, we were never allowed to know." He looks over at me with a forced smile. "We can come back if you'd like, walk around, and get a bit closer."

"What was that phone call about?" He looks straight ahead, no emotion betrayed.

"Nothing for you to worry about." His mouth is set in a hard line.

"Rhys, stop keeping things from me. Talk to me, please." A deep sigh marks his partial resignation.

"It was a reporter, Sophie, wanting a story." Shaking his head, he reaches over and grabs my hand. "Can we please not talk about it?" I want to talk about it. What story? I am tired of always feeling like I am in the dark, but I can see in the set of his jaw that he really doesn't want to broach the subject any further, and I decide to revisit.

"Where are we going?" We crest a deep green hill and come to look upon a wide, spread valley with the rolling river meandering across the landscape, in the distance I can see the mist rising from what must be a waterfall or rapids, and on the other side of the river sits a long, stone building. As we get closer, I notice the letters SFS written in contrasting color roof tiles topping the building. I look over to Rhys only to catch him smiling for the first time all day. He is beaming. We come to stop in front of the main building; craggy gray stones that look hundreds of years old, arched windows with aged wooden shutters freshly painted a bright green to match the landscape, and tall smoke stacks with pyres of pure white steam rising into the clear blue sky.

He holds my hand as we walk the length of the building to a wide barn door that sits half open. He pulls the heavy doors open to reveal an expansive space filled by copper kettles surrounded by cat walks and scaffolding.

"Is this yours?" I ask in awe, still not totally sure what I'm looking at, but impressed by the sheer scale nevertheless.

"One of my investments," he winks as we weave through kettles and walk towards the back of the building. "It's a family business, actually William's brainchild. I'm just the checkbook and the taste tester," he grins. We spend most of the day at the still with William giving us the tour, explaining, mostly to me, how the whiskey is made.

He takes us out to another building that is dark and sealed off and cool, where the walls are lined with row after row of wooden barrels all filled with the family whiskey at various stages of aging. Rhys is ecstatic, soaking everything in, beaming with pride and enthusiasm.

Through another open barn door, I come across a small field populated with goats. It seems odd until I look further and notice a wide spread mini farm that appears to encompass the property. The goats run free as well as a few colorful roosters, some quietly pecking hens and a gaggle of geese that seem to waddle aimlessly but always in a tight group.

"This is all Colleen," William grins with pride as he talks about his sister. "She said, *'Why don't we grow our own barley?'* The little trickster talked me out of half the land and here we are two years later looking to expand. She has a bake shop and country store on the other side of the property. She treats those silly goats like family, but she makes some delicious cheeses and bakes like a wizard. You should take Sophie over there once we are done here." He nudges Rhys, and leads us into a smaller out building that is smoky, but oddly cool.

More casks line the walls, smaller and of darker wood than the others, and between each row there are wheels of cheese. Sides of pig hang from the rafters in the middle of the small building between two open fire pits in the stone floor.

Flames rise from the pits, reaching for the curing meats. Finn appears with a barrel grasped within the jaws of a massive pair of steel tongs. His forearms bulge as he lifts the barrel above the fire and slowly lowers it, swallowing the flames and the smoke. He releases the jaws of the tongs and steps back, smiling and nodding at Rhys.

"I'm smoking my wood!" he calls over the barrel with a wicked grin, before he closes the tongs around the barrel and pulls it off the fire, flipping it over, and putting it down. He pumps a metal pedal on the floor and the flames are tamed, retreating into the pit. He steps over it and reaches out to shake Rhys' hand. "Welcome to my cooperage, Cousin."

They talk barrels as we are guided through the remainder of the still before we walk down the hill and visit Colleen in her little shop. The finished hams are wrapped and hung on the front porch.

Brigid's jams line the little front window. The produce from the farm is strewn about in hand woven baskets, as are loaves of Irish bread and little wheels of goat cheese, some rolled in ash, others covered with vibrant herbs, and the rest a luscious creamy pure white, a little slice of heaven on earth.

"The smartest investment is always family," he whispers from behind, wrapping his arms around me and pulling me close. "Look at what she has done in such a short time. She wants to expand into agritourism."

"I think that's a fantastic idea. When I thought of Ireland, this is what I pictured, this is what I wanted to see and feel. It's perfect. Why are you smiling like that?" His gleeful smirk is a most welcome sight.

"You glow when you're so happy. I'm so glad I could bring you here; that I could see all of this with you by my side, Sophie. I love you and I want you happy just like this." He kisses my temple and holds me in a warm embrace and for that moment I am happy.

CH. 12

Driving back towards the farm his mood starts to plummet and mine is pulled down in tandem. Surrounded by all this beauty and all I can feel is his unexplained melancholy and the need to alleviate whatever it is that is pulling him down.

Colleen is bustling around the kitchen when we return and I opt to stay and help her prep for supper while Rhys takes a nap, and I hope sleep will lighten his mood. After about an hour and two dozen peeled potatoes, I head to our room but find Rhys nowhere. I explore the floor and find him in a small corner room that's darker and cooler than the rest. He lies on a little metal framed double bed, flat on his back, his arms flung over his head. His mouth is slack, eyes still closed, his chest rises slightly with each shallow breath.

Panels of gauze are flung over the curtain rods in front of the arched windows and I'm suddenly inspired. I pull a swath of gauze from the rod and step up next to the bed. His eyes flutter and I seize an opportunity. I climb over him and straddle his hips, knowing he is still too weak to really fight back and too sleepy to be quick. We are going to solve this mood, whatever it takes. He looks up at me with those deep green eyes, his long dark lashes fluttering, trying to bat the sleep away as he narrows his gaze to my low slung shirt. His eyes rise for a split second as my breasts swing free beneath the clingy white cotton. I lean forward, brushing across his face before I grab his hands and quickly pull them above his head. Before he can catch his breath and see past my breasts, I snake the gauze around one wrist and wind it around the flimsy metal bed frame and close it with a knot around his other wrist. He jerks against the restraint and growls at me as I climb off of his chest and stand next to the tiny bed. It creaks and groans under his weight. The paint is chipping off the corner showing layer after layer of color that hides a rusty, hollow steel frame. I stand and watch as a slow smile spreads across his face and his crooked grin nearly lights my body on fire. He raises an eyebrow at me, begging for an explanation.

"You have been very grumpy and I am tired of it. I want you to snap out of it."

"And you thought this would help?" The timbre of his voice flows through me like honey slow and viscous, thick with sinful sugar and raw, unfiltered lust. I unsnap my jeans and work them over my hips, watching his eyes flare. Slowly I slide the rough denim down my legs until they drop at my feet. I slide off my panties and ball the small patch of pink silk into my hand. A lazy breeze licks across my exposed skin, sending a shiver running across my shoulders and I pull my shirt down over my hips careful not to expose myself to him. Climbing over him, he tugs at the scarf as a show of protest, but it's clear his heart is not in it. He is happily along for the ride so I better commit. I slide up on his chest and sit just inches from his face. His mouth falls open, releasing a deep gasp, the faint pulse of his heart and the rumble from his breathing echoes deep in my belly. I tuck my feet behind me and rest my knees on either side of his head, pressed against his ears. I can do this.

His tongue slowly rolls across his lips up and over the curve of his mouth. I can feel it all over, but I resist the urge to melt into a puddle right on his chest. I lean back and pull the shirt up around my hips, exposing my brazenly bald, smooth as silk, freshly shaved pussy to his ravenous gaze.

"Oh my God, what have you done? Come closer," he whispers. I shake my head and smile as he lifts his head, stretching to reach my pulsing center. His tongue darts from between his lips, straining to make contact with my bare flesh. Watching him hungry and unable to satiate himself is strangely satisfying. His eyes grow wide as I slide my hand down my stomach and brush across the top of the smooth skin. Like the petal of a rose, the flesh is like velvet. I brush my fingers across my slit and sink into the pooling slickness overflowing from my lips. I rock my hips back, spreading myself across his flesh as he moans in delight.

"Come closer," his whisper is more urgent this time. "Let me taste you," I nod in response and continue to pet my pussy, watching him go crazy. The bare skin warms under my touch as blood rises to the surface, casting a pretty pink flush under my puffy flesh. My fingertip rolls across my clit and I jump. "Come closer," he demands, craning his neck, tugging at his restraints. Frustration and lust flare in his eyes. "Come closer, Sophie!" he growls, bucking his hips, trying to force me onto his face. As I work my pussy with one hand, I close my other fist around the balled up panties and quickly shove them into his open mouth.

"Shhhh," I tease. His eyes bulge in shock and then flash in delight. "The time for talking is over." Lowering his head to the pillow in resignation, he takes a deep breath and sighs. Looking down on him I am shocked at my own boldness, and more than a little turned on by my own power. This powerful, sexual man, tied to a tiny child's bed with my panties shoved into his mouth at my mercy. The power is intoxicating. He tugs against his restraints again, pulling me from my self-discovery.

"I will let you taste me, Mr. Slate, if you are a good boy and do as I say. Can you do that?" I find it hard to keep a straight face, but bite back the grin and wait for a sign from him. He narrows his eyes at me, his dark brows dipping over his smoky eyes. I smile sweetly as he nods and takes a deep breath beneath me. I swipe my fingers across my begging clit again and cannot fight back the little moans that

accompany the circles I make over my slick sex.
His nose flares and his hungry eyes devour the sight
as I dip my middle finger between the folds and into
the heat. Slowly I slide my finger into my pussy and
then out, just resting against my entrance, glistening
with the pulse of my desire. I pull my finger from
my body and rest it across his lips that remain
wrapped around my silk panties. He closes his eyes
and breathes deeply through his nose, taking me all
in.

I slip away from him and slide down his body,
leaving a trail of warm wet kisses down one side of
his stunning, chiseled torso and up the other. His
skin is paler than usual; the horrid bruises are
quickly fading, leaving behind a slight green cast.
The angry scar across his hip has softened but not
faded, raised to the touch, a forever reminder of the
accident. I place a soft kiss at the center of the scar,
running my tongue along the ridge. He flinches
beneath me and shifts. I slide to the side and move
between his legs. Grasping the waistband of his
pants I pull them from his body, tossing them to the
floor. He raises his head as I sink between his legs
and our eyes meet. I run my hands up his powerful
thighs and draw circles with my thumbs. His eyes
are begging; begging for me to suck him, dying for
me to take him into my mouth and lick him like a
lollipop. And I plan on doing just that. I tease him
mercilessly, running my tongue up the delicate flesh

of his thigh, circling around the base of his growing cock and gliding back down the other side. Over and over I labor to hypnotize him with the repetition until he moans so beautifully and drops his head to the pillow.

As a reward I lick over the slit of his cock, teasing the tip before I sink my hungry lips over his steely length. Like velvet against my tongue, the skin of his dick is soft and sweet. I sink over him until he is pressed to the back of my throat, and then slowly slide off of him, blowing a stream of cool air over his tight wet skin. An echoing shiver slithers up his body as I take him back into my mouth and begin to bob slowly. Pushing him to the back of my throat over and over, I run my tongue along the smooth skin of his shaft and cup his balls, rolling them around in my hand. He groans and I pump faster, sucking his flesh, pulling him deeper into my mouth until he twitches and seizes his legs around me.

He is struggling for control, trying to stop the great white wave that threatens to overcome him, but I want it. I suck him back into my mouth with a great slurp and sink down to the root. My tongue slides across the base of his pulsing cock and I tickle the delicate skin of his balls. With two great pumps with my ferocious mouth and a gentle tug on his tight sack, he has no choice but to empty himself. Violently he thrusts his hips upward, plunging his angry cock down my throat as he erupts into a white hot pulse, coating my throat.

I look up at him, still licking his lust from my lips and he just nods, ecstasy clouding his eyes. I crawl up his body, tasting every inch as I go, his warm skin heaven to my swollen lips. He moans and the sound sends my heart racing. I rest my knees on each side of his head and look down into his face. A slow grin spreads across those lips and I lower myself onto his warm, waiting mouth. He starts slowly, running his velvet tongue the length of my pussy, back and forth until I'm lulled and comfortable and I forget myself, forget everything and just start riding his face. There is nothing else but tongue, teeth and lips; my heat and throbbing little clit that trembles with excitement each time his tongue rolls around the center of the universe. I reach down and cradle his head, pulling him into me. His tongue plunges into me over and over, the hypnotic rhythm building and pushing me upwards.

I'm reminded of his restraints when he tugs and the whole bed moves as he struggles against the ties. He is rabid and wild, fucking me with his face as he pulls at the gauze and I reach down and free him. His hands grip my thighs, his fingertips digging delightfully into my skin as he grinds his face against me, devouring me gladly. My hips undulate of their own accord and I ride hard until the wave crests and all the blood drains from my extremities and shoots straight to my pulsing clit that's perched on the edge of an abyss.

He sucks that writhing bundle of nerves between his glistening lips and I fall, throwing my head back. I pray for salvation as he pulls me against him, but he does not relent. He licks and nips and suckles at my core until he has had his fill and I am exhausted, barely able to hold my head up when he finally loosens his grip on my thighs. I am limp and boneless, still catching my breath as I slide down his body and rest my head on his chest. He whispers and coos in my ear, but I hardly hear a thing, more aware of his warm breath and the strong beat of his heart.

"You really taught me a lesson, Sophie." I lazily turn my head to see his dimpled grin.

"No more work," I barely mumble.

"No more work," he relents, kissing the top of my head. We must have fallen asleep because the next thing I know I'm shivering and curling against him in the dark, waking to the sound of the family gathered around the fire in the courtyard.

CH. 13

In no time at all I fall into the easy rhythm of Rhys' family life. Morning in the yard with Brigid and Colleen, afternoons tooling around the countryside, watching Rhys reconnect and network for the future of his family. Back and forth from the still the boys come and go, most, but not all; Michael and Colleen have their own agendas all together, but in true Slate family fashion, are equally important investments that Rhys nurtures and encourages.

After almost a week, he finally seems at ease as if the rest of the world has just fallen away and left us to this small piece of heaven.

We spend a Saturday evening at a pub in Tulla with his cousins and they are rowdy. It seems half the village is packed into the small stone pub. A group of fiddle players sits in the corner, keeping the crowd entertained. Children dance while their parents eat and visit. Beer flows and conversation sparkles as it seems there are no strangers in the building. The sense of community is comforting and contagious. The music picks up as the crowd thins out and the families take their early leave. I couldn't count how many more rounds the boys made it through before they gave in and called it a night, but when the bartender rang the bell there was no choice.

"Ye don't have to go home, but ye can't stay

here!" When we finally spill out of the pub and onto the cobbled streets, Rhys is grinning ear to ear, Michael is trying to pick a fight with someone who seems all too familiar with his patterns, and William is sidling up to one of the few remaining girls, working all too hard for nothing in return. I admire the window dressings of the small shops on the street while the boys begin to sing and holler until I hear Colleen and the distinct rumble of that old pickup truck pounding its way across the cobblestones.

HONK! She lays on the horn and gives them all a startle.

"Aye, hop in you rowdy lot before I leave ye here on the street and ye can walk back!" They start to file towards the truck with Rhys moving for the passenger door.

"Oh no, ladies in the front, you sods can air out in the back. Come along, Sophie!" she yells to me as Rhys shoots her a look before flashing a grin to me and rolling into the back with the others. I hop in the cab and we head out of town and back into the country. I wonder how many of these drives Colleen has done, how much of this Rhys misses when he is not here.

When we finally pull into the drive, the men are more sedate and file off in the direction of their respective rooms. I follow Rhys into the kitchen and watch him pour himself a glass of water.

"I may have drank a bit much," he says with a grin and a slight sway.

"You think?" I wrap my arms around his waist and kiss his neck.

"It's that damn William, always having to best me, always having to push. I can't let him win. Never could."

"No, I imagine that would be the end of the world," I tease as his hands skate down my sides.

"I'm starting to feel like myself again, Sophie," his lips graze my collar bone and send a spark down my body. "Now, I'd like to feel you." He cups my ass in his hands and pulls me into him, pressing his body to mine.

"I believe you have a handful right now," I tease and kiss his neck, moving towards his ear. "Take me upstairs," I whisper.

"Gladly." He drops his glass in the sink and grabs my hand, pulling me behind him, up the stairs and along the darkened corridor.

It is frantic and hot. He is drunk and mad with lust and I relish every drop of his ferocious attentions. He sinks his teeth into my flesh and groans with such delight it sends me reeling. I buck against him wildly, fingers tangling in his hair, holding on while he tears into me. Flipping me over he slaps my ass so hard his hand print is sure to remain. We can't get close enough; our bodies are slick with sweat, skin clinging and sticky from the heat. I could drink every last drop of him, and the thirst would remain unquenchable.

The sun assaults my eyes only moments before the damn rooster does, crowing to the morning, calling us all to wake. I roll over to find Rhys gone and I stretch across the narrow bed, allowing my body to come awake on its own. The sun is warm on my skin, but the air that hovers around me is chilled and sets my body at attention. I climb out of bed and pull on a pair of pants before heading downstairs.

What I come upon is not what I was expecting. The morning bustle is dialed up. There are piles of potatoes covering the counter top and Colleen stands with her hip against the counter, tea in hand, watching as Michael and Charlie carry in two huge packages of something wrapped in butcher paper slung over each of their shoulders. In a rehearsed move, they both sling their package to the table with a heavy thud and peel the paper back. Brigid moves in to inspect what they have brought.

"Very nice boys and fine butchering, Michael. This should turn out beautifully, put her out on the spit and mind the coals. I'll be going to dress now. The rest of ye should do the same." She turns to me and pats my cheek, "I hope ye brought something for church." Breezing by with a jovial air, she calls behind her as she ascends the steps, "Our Lord waits for no man remember."

Colleen watches me as I move closer to the table to peek at what the boys have brought. I look up to see her grinning ear to ear.

"Lamb," she says with a wink, placing her teacup next to the sink and wiping her hands on her apron. "It's Feasting Day, Sophie, The Feast of Our Lady."

She moves around the table inspecting Michael's work. Rhys walks in followed by William, Patrick and Finn. In each of their hands dangle lifeless chickens, relieved of their feathers. Rhys drops the chickens on the butcher block and comes for me, hands outstretched, covered in dirt, and blood, and tiny feathers. I back away and his eyes light up.

He lunges for me and I turn to run almost knocking Patrick down. This gives me a head start and I take the steps two at a time while Rhys gets around Finn and is close on my heels. He's got a definite spring in his step and mischief on his face. I rush into our room and he shuts the door behind me, shoulders crouching, as he rounds me like a lion tamer.

"Don't do anything you'll regret," he winks. "I've got feathers and I'm not afraid to use them."

I back slowly into the bathroom and start the shower for him, hoping for a show. When he catches me watching, he hams it up by turning his back, throwing a seductively, silly look over his shoulder.

"You like what you see?" he purrs theatrically and I burst out laughing as he drops his shorts, quickly squelching my amusement and catching my attention for more carnal reasons.

"You're very spirited this morning," I tease as he pops the button on my jeans and pulls them down around my ankles.

"Step," he commands. I step out of them and he kicks them to the side, quickly disposing of my panties. Pulling my shirt over my head, he stands, backing me into the tiny stone shower. The warm water washes over my face as we come to stand beneath the shower head, eye to eye, all humor gone. He swiftly lathers his body and mine in thick suds before dropping the soap to the stone floor. He kisses me, water mingling with our tongues, washing over us, trickling into my mouth.

"We don't have much time," he pulls away, taking my breath with him, sinking to his knees before me. "We have to go to church." Grabbing my leg, he hitches it over his shoulder, sinking his teeth into my thigh. Rivers of suds flow down his powerful back and I am mesmerized by the landscape of his body.

"Church?" I gasp as his fingers slip into my eager pussy.

"The Feast of Our Lady," he mouths, licking my excitement from his fingers, "and now to feast on *my* lady." He buries his face in my wanting flesh, parting my lips with his strong fingers, opening me up. The warm water and his tongue dance over my clit and I close my eyes resting my head against the stone. He pulls my clit into his mouth, claiming my slick pussy with his fingers. He slides his fingers to the knuckles and pumps his hands furiously, knocking loose an indescribable force. My cunt erupts and I start to scream. I have no control, my body flapping against the stone, unable to battle wave after violent wave that racks my body. He stands and swiftly replaces his fingers with his cock. Hooking his arms under my legs, he pulls me from my toes and presses me against the wall. He holds me open and pillages my body with animalistic thrusts that take my breath away.

Water drips from his brow, his wild eyes are fixed on me, determined, as he pounds me into the stone. At this point I'm merely an instrument that he plays expertly, holding me aloft as he slides his raging cock in and out of my greedy body. He speeds up, closing his eyes, his neck stretched to the ceiling. I watch the water run in rivulets down his neck and take one on my tongue. Licking his warm, pulsing flesh from the base of his neck, I pull his ear between my teeth before his shoulders tense and his movements slow, becoming deliberate and measured. His eyes are alight with determination, but wild, a growing orgasm clouding his focus. He bends his knees and we dip before he thrusts into me, filling every empty space with his heat before he erupts. I shortly follow him on a rolling pulse that radiates from our meeting point and spreads like a wave of wild fire.

"Hmmm," he hums in my ear as he sets my feet to the ground, contentment rich in his gaze. He dips and kisses me gently as my senses are still creeping back and he turns me around. I press my face to the cool stone as he washes my hair, taking me closer to heaven than I've ever been. Love pours from his fingers as he rinses my hair and slowly turns me to face him.

Between the cloud of lust that still hangs between us and the warm water sliding down my body, I'm floating and hardly conscious of anything, but Rhys. Caressing me with his strong hands, pushes the remaining suds from my body and rinses me clean before turning the water on him. He turns and I wash his back, taking special care with my favorite spots. He tips his head to the ceiling with a grunt and a wicked grin.

"No more time for that, Beautiful," he hums, "the family is waiting." He kisses me and turns the water off. Cold air assaults us both immediately and he grabs for a towel, wrapping it around my shoulders, before grabbing the other and wrapping it about his waist.

We dress quickly and he explains The Feast of

Our Lady and what the day has in store. First, we
will all attend church as a family and then most of
the parish will be coming to the farm for a feast. I
am excited about the prospect of a proper Irish
feast, but nervous about going to church with his
family to a traditional Irish Catholic Church. When
I used to go with Lola, I never paid much attention.
Catholic was my culture, but not my religion.

I blow my hair dry, leaving it loose before
pulling out the only church appropriate stitch of
clothing I brought; the simple black jersey dress that
Liv insisted on packing. *Thank you, Olivia.* I watch
Rhys button his crisp, white shirt that Brigid surely
ironed for him. He slips a tartan waistcoat over his
shoulders and drops a gold watch in the pocket. I
button his vest for him and kiss him swiftly on the
neck before slipping into a pair of flats. He sweeps
me into his arms and kisses me senseless before
pulling me down the stairs.

The kitchen is deserted, but the courtyard is
raucous when we step out into the morning sun. The
boys are standing around shouting orders at Charlie,
who is stacking wood for the fire all by himself.
They all wear the same vest and I can't help but
grin at the way they all look like a band of merry
ruffians, bonded by blood and tradition and tartan.
Colleen and Brigid stand in the shade of the willow,
watching, tea length dresses perfectly pressed, lace
shawls around their shoulders. Rhys joins in the

zealous supervision and I join the ladies in the shade.

"You look lovely, Sophie," Brigid looks me up and down in approval, "but, something is missing. I have a gift for you, dear. Come with me." I follow Brigid into the house and through the kitchen. She pulls a small wooden box from a closet and lays it open on the table. Inside lays delicate white lace that looks handmade and very old; the pattern is intricate and beautiful. She picks it up and unfolds it. It's larger than I thought, the size of a shawl, just like the shawl that she and Colleen are wearing, yet, hers is black.

"This was my mother's, Rhys' grandmother's. It has been passed down for many generations. We all have a stitch in it and now I would like you to have it." I take a step back in disbelief.

"I can't accept this, Brigid, it's a family heirloom, besides, I wouldn't even know what to do with it," I respond, still not sure even what the lace is for.

"Well," she begins, forcibly turning me around and swiping my hair off my shoulders, "you are going to wear it to church this morning, to begin with. This is a chapel veil. It is our job to maintain tradition, Sophie; to pass down our way of life, to honor those that have come before us who built the foundations that we continue to build upon. Your Rhys is a builder. He makes a good name for this family and makes us all proud. I am proud of him for loving you, Sophie. You belong around our table, you belong here. This is our way." She drapes the veil over my head and straightens it over my hair, making sure it spills over my shoulders. The moment she sets it upon my head, I feel the weight of the lace, heavy with the past. "The veil shows you are humble, my dear, it shows your reverence for the Lord and your thankfulness for this life and I'll be proud for you to have it." She pinches my cheeks and pats my face with a tear in her eye. Before it can fall she turns away and calls for me to follow.

"Let's get on, you lot. We don't want to keep Our Lady waiting." The whole family files out the bright red gate and down a winding path that leads down a hill and away from the farm. Rhys takes my hand and we fall back a few steps behind the rest of the family.

CH. 14

"You look positively ethereal, my love." He squeezes my hand, rolling his fingers across the palm of my hand, back and forth, lulling me into comfort. "I am so happy you are here, Sophie." As we crest a small hill the church comes into view and I stop dead in my tracks. People are filing into the small stone church from all directions and it takes my breath away. I'm moved by the scene; the little old church, the people, the landscape. I can't believe I am here. It's all so surreal, like a scene from The Quiet Man. A slow happy tear trickles down my cheek before I can get a hold of my emotions. Rhys swipes it away with his thumb, raising it to his mouth. "I hope those are tears of joy?"

I shake my head back and forth, unable to form the words. It's all just too beautiful, too quaint, and too real. I can't remember the last time I felt so overwhelmed with a sense of peace and happiness. It's like Deja vu, as if I've been here before, like returning to a home I've never known.

As we file into the church, Brigid greets every smiling face and tells anyone willing to listen about me and Rhys. The women kiss his cheeks and the men shake his hand, praising him and welcoming him home. I play with the lace to calm my nerves, running it through my fingers as I'm introduced to seemingly everyone in the church

The nave of the church is more stunning than the outside lead me to believe. Beautiful stained glass windows cast a rainbow of light across the pews and illuminate a beautiful stone statue of The Virgin Mary holding the Baby Jesus. Brigid leads the family right to the front and we occupy two narrow pews. She kneels immediately and lowers her head in prayer, as does Colleen. I slide from the bench onto my knees and do the same, thanking God for bringing Rhys into my life, for bringing me here. I close my eyes and absorb the sounds around me, parishioners greeting one another, the creaking of the old wooden benches, and the squeals of small children.

I struggle to understand the ceremony as the Father speaks with a strong accent and slips in and out of Gaelic. When the time comes for communion Brigid insists I go with her to receive the sacrament. I haven't had communion since I was a small girl. The bishop places the wafer on my outstretched tongue and makes the sign of the cross before I step over to Father O'Brien and he tips the golden goblet to my lips. When I turn, Rhys' radiant smile fills me with pride and peace. I walk back to the pew, kneel and close my eyes in silent thanks as the rest of the church receives their communion.

After Mass everyone congregates outside to visit and talk about the feast. Rhys pulls me around the side of the gray stone building, pushing me up against the cool, rough stone.

"Is it wrong that it made my cock hard watching you take communion?" He presses himself against me, his lips sweeping across my throat. I swat at his arm in feigned shock.

"Yes, it is wrong, you deviant." I giggle as he slips his hand between my legs, cupping my sinfully wet pussy while his warm mouth brushes against my ear.

"When was your last confession?" He pulls my panties to the side and begins to slowly stroke my velveteen skin. My pulse spikes as he slips a finger in my eager pussy and starts to pump.

"Aye, Cousin! The Lord is watching!" Finn catcalls as he comes closer, his eyes firmly fixed on me.

"Aye, and so are you, cad. Now divert your eyes before I blacken them," Rhys returns, sliding his hands from between my legs and turning to shelter me from Finn's libidinous gaze. Finn laughs and slaps Rhys' shoulder.

"No need for threats, dear Cousin. Just trying to save you from the wolves, better me that finds ye than Ma, and she is ready to go." I smooth my skirt as Rhys reaches for my hand and we head back to the farm, our walking party significantly larger on the return trip.

The feast starts innocently enough with families and frolicking children. The older generation sits around watching as the young men play a game of Rounders and the young girls watch in awe and giggle. The party lasts well into the morning hours, although the prayer and reverence ended when the sun went down. We dance and sing, drink copious amounts of whiskey and beer, eat until every bone is picked clean and talk until there is nothing left to say.

As the party fades into memory, embers of the slowly dying bonfire mingle with the early morning sun as it crests the hills and lights a new day. The chickens peck the ground searching for scraps as the boys clear the yard. Rhys tends the smallest fire, keeping it alive for Brigid to make breakfast, while the others are doused. The last neighbors trickle out, stretching their goodbyes and thanking Brigid for the feast, carrying baskets of leftovers with a few fresh eggs and a jar of her coveted jam.

I wrap the lace shawl around me in protection from

the cool morning breeze that whips through the trees while I watch Rhys. William steps up next to me, wrapping his burly arm around my shoulder, tugging me to his side.

"You did well, Lass." He smiles with a twinkle in his eye, "I didn't think you had it in you, didn't think you could last." His booming laughter catches Rhys' attention and he watches as William pulls me closer and whispers in my ear.

"You make him happy, I like that. You make my Ma happy, I like that more. You're a good girl Sophie Noelle. Welcome to the family." He squeezes me and places a perfunctory kiss atop my head before practically pushing me away and stomping over to Rhys. I can't help the surely stupid grin that paints my face, and the no doubt stunning shade of pink from blushing so deeply at his approval.

They slap each other on the back and embrace before it devolves into a wrestling match, lasting only a few short moments before Brigid appears with a frying pan and shoos them away from the fire. We all circle around as Finn places more wood on the fire and the heat from the sun and the fire mingle.

Colleen comes out with a tray of mugs and puts a kettle on the coals. We watch the farm come to life, the sun moving across the sky while we eat and drink and reminisce about the night's events. The sun sits high before my body protests and I have to sleep. Rhys and I are the first to leave the fire and head to bed, but the rest soon follow as the noise in the courtyard dies down. I lay exhausted in the most heavenly place on earth, Rhys' arms.

"I think it's time we go home, Beautiful." His words float across my mind as I close my weary eyes.

"I never want to go home." I can barely get the

words out before I fall headlong into a deep, sated sleep.

CH. 15

He calls Nina first thing when we wake to fill her in on our travel arrangements. I wander down to the fire, still slowly smoldering with a kettle nestled in the coals. Colleen hands me a cup and fills it with hot water before she starts gathering dishes to be brought inside. I take a quick sip of tea and follow her around the yard, helping her gather the last remnants of yesterday's festivities.

"Rhys says you are heading home soon. Do you live in New York, too?"

"I don't." Rhys appears in the doorway, looking at me with undefined expectations. "I live in Colorado, or rather, I lived in Colorado. Now I guess I'm just a wanderer," I smile. "I don't really have a home base now that my grandmother is gone. I had always hoped to hold on to her house and live there, but now that the house is gone, I'm not sure what to do. I don't feel connected. I think when we get back I'll start looking for a job and see where the wind takes me."

"So, the house sold?" Rhys asks inquisitively, tipping his tea to his lips, keeping his eyes fixed on me.

"It did. It went to auction last week. Mary sent me the notice of sale." A knot twists in my heart at the thought of someone else living in Lola's house, the house my grandfather's hands built, the house my dad grew up in, the house that I believed would always be my home. "It's done." I swear his mouth twists in a grin, but I can't believe he would take any pleasure in my pain.

"Why doesn't she move in with you, Rhys?" My pulse spikes at her recommendation, my face feels like it just caught fire and my palms are cold and sweaty. He just smiles and tosses the rest of his tea down his throat before turning and disappearing up the steps. My heart sinks to the cold stone floor; there's an answer if ever silence was one. He doesn't want me to live with him, not that I want it or have even thought about it, but hell, no response, that's not what I expected.

"I'm sorry, Sophie, did I say something wrong?"

"No, Colleen, it's ok. We've just never talked about that." I smile sweetly and tend to the dishes that she piles in the sink. I spend the afternoon with her tending the chicks and listening to her plans for the farm.

For hours there is no sight of Rhys.

We gather around the fire as the sun begins to sink behind emerald hills and he finally appears again, an apparition, my ghost. I try to push the hurt away from earlier, his rejection by silence. He walks up behind me and wraps his arms around me, laying a manila envelope across my lap.

"What's this?"

"It's *our* future," he whispers in my ear before wandering a few paces away, eyeing me intently. "It arrived a few days ago. I was going to wait until we got home," he tips his eyebrow at me, "but now seems like an opportune time. Open it."

I slide a thick stack of clearly legal paperwork from the envelope. **Transfer of Title** is scrolled across the top, followed by my grandmother's address. I look up at Rhys, at the rest of the family watching me, waiting for some prescribed reaction, but I return to the stack and keep reading. I scan the page and find Rhys' signature as the Guarantor, Nina's signature as the Witness, and a few lines down in an addendum, there's my name, listed under Sole Property Owner, Sophie Rose Noelle, Owner.

Every moment I have ever had in that house flashes behind my eyes, all of us crowded into her tiny kitchen at Christmas, Easter egg hunts in the backyard, parade mornings filled with coffee and donuts and wandering neighbors. I catch a sob in my throat and swallow it back; fighting the fog that so happily shades my vision. Through the fire I see his shining face, beaming with anticipation, with pride, with love. In my hands is the one thing I thought I always wanted, yet from the moment I heard he was in that accident, I had hardly given it a second thought. I had chalked it up to a loss that I would move past, to a sentimental dream that wasn't meant to be, and now I hold it in my hands; the deed to my family's past, the link to the one thing I have left.

I'm reminded of those around me by the warmth of Rhys' hand on my shoulder. I have an iron grip on the papers pressed firmly to my breast, cradled and protected, possessive. He helps me up and we wander away from the fire, away from the gaze of his family. My white knuckle grip does not relax as we loop around the yard and through the red gate, heading towards the open barn.

"I can't believe you did this," the hoarse whisper barely passes my lips before he swings me around and kisses my happily tear stained mouth.

"I would do anything to see you smile like that again, Beautiful, anything." With the papers pressed between us, we sway in the twilight of the evening, his arms wound tightly around me.

"Will you invite me over?" he murmurs, brushing his lips across my throat.

"How can I say no to the man who bought me a house?" He teases me with his tongue before stepping back and looking me dead in the eye.

"Don't worry," he reaches out and tucks a rogue curl behind my ear, "you'll earn it, Sophie." That dimple breaks across his cheek and I swear my flesh catches fire.

I move closer to him, running my free hand down his chest and purr, "Yes, I'll earn it." I pull his ear between my teeth and press myself to him, waiting for his arms to snake around me in that way that says I belong to him, but he holds me at bay.

"You will earn it, Sophie." I take a step back and study his face, stone with the exception of an almost imperceptible twitch at the corner of his sinful mouth. I take another glance at the papers and put on my best professional face before sliding them safely back into the envelope.

"Yes, I will earn it." I take a step closer and tip my chin, barely meeting his eyes. "I'll do whatever you want," I whisper, offering myself to him.

"I know you will, Beautiful," he growls, pulling me closer, our bodies melding, pulses meeting, racing neck and neck. "I have a job for you." His voice is serious before turning smug, "*you'll see where the wind takes you*?" he snorts. The audacity of his dismay is charming and I quietly love his need to assert himself.

"I *am* the wind, Sophie, and I will take you any way I like." He pushes the barn door all the way back, pushing me up against it. "Do not drop those papers." His eyes are black as coal and there's a devious curl to his mouth. My pulse spikes as his hands run down my sides before he pulls me to him, his fingers hooked in my waistband. In the space of a breath, my pants are around my ankles and his eyes flash with glee. He slowly sinks to his knees taking my panties with him all the way to the dirt. A cool wind licks at my pussy and I gasp in anticipation of his warm mouth.

He sits back on his heels and watches me tremble and writhe in the breeze like a wanton leaf dancing towards the ground. Charlie's booming voice carries over from the fire and I freeze, suddenly so aware of my exposure.

Rhys stands, throwing me over his shoulder, my bare ass high in the air, my ankles bound by my jeans, my hands still holding on to the papers. A deep chuckle rumbles us both before he swings me back to my feet just inside the barn, backed up against the open door. The truck is gone and the barn is empty but for a few bales of hay and some rusty old parts.

"Better?" he asks, backing away to get a better look. "Spread your legs," he demands, not waiting for an answer, flicking his fingers to the side. I open my legs as wide as my denim shackles will allow and he moves closer. At my feet, he drops his face inches away from my open pussy, his hands firmly gripping his thighs. He blows across my flesh, sending a rattle down my spine, my hands tremble

"Hold those papers above your head." His voice is quiet, but forceful, and I obey without hesitation. With my arms stretched above me, he slides between my legs; his hands branding the inside of my thighs, his breath making me ache. He teases and taunts, his fingers barely grazing my skin. My arms sag and my hips start to undulate in desperation as he looks up at me.

"Keep your arms above your head, Beautiful. I want you to focus, can you do that?" I take a deep breath and look into his eyes, feeling nothing but the overwhelming need to do just as he says, as if his tone is the very switch. As I raise my arms high above my head, he slips a finger deep into my warm pussy and I am relieved. I let my head fall back and I close my eyes, papers held high in the air with my pants around my ankles. A single strong finger slides between my silky lips and I ache for more.

He rises to meet my eyes, his fingers never leaving my pussy. His eyes flare with each thrust and I drown in his intense gaze. He grasps my face in his other hand, demanding my full attention.

"You are not alone, Sophie," he pants. "You will never be alone again, I will take care of you. You just have to let me." I drop the papers to the dirt and tear at his belt, desperate to free him, to swallow him whole, shredding my fingertips.

He puts his foot between my legs and lifts me, leaving my shoes and jeans in a pile on the ground. With his hands under my arms I lift myself and wrap my legs around his waist as he pushes his pants out of the way. His cock springs free between us, strong and hard, my pussy calling to him like a siren and he wastes no time. Lifting me away from his body slightly, he places himself at the center of my raging inferno and presses me against the rough barn wall as he slides the length of his cock into me so slowly I may just go mad. Back and forth he swings his hips, building to a frantic pace. Our bodies slap together, hips crashing into one another. I ride him as he bucks his hips against me, his strong fingers bruising my thighs as he claims me in the dull light if the barn. When he meets his end the most delightfully raw growl escapes his throat and echoes from the worn old wood.

"Mine!". Like a wolf howling at the moon he is lost and the sound quietly pushes me over the edge. My pussy drips around him as the warm, wild timber of his voice carries over the sounds of a fading day. His wild eyes find mine and we watch each other come down from the clouds, connected by sight, by body, by mind.

"You'll never be alone, Sophie."

Our last two days on the farm pass in a flash. Bridget made Rhys promise to bring me back quickly and I promised Colleen that I would work on Rhys and garner her an invitation to visit as soon as possible. Saying goodbye to Rhys' family was like saying goodbye to my own, and left a small hole in my heart.

A quiet sadness filled the car as we drove away from the farm, the brothers calling behind us for safe travels. Before I know it, we are back to reality. The lights of New York City twinkle below us like a beacon, calling us home, back to the ravages of the city, and into the clutches of Nadja.

CH. 16

Charlie slips easily back into his expected role as driver and guides us through late night traffic and I rest my head on Rhys' shoulder as we circumnavigate the city.

A shadowy figure hangs on the rail of Rhys' stoop when we pull up to his building. Charlie stops the car and begins to unload the bags, ever watchful. Rhys turns to me, the worry on his face almost shadowed by the dark of the night.

"Stay in the car, Sophie."

"Who is that?"

"Just stay in the car, promise me." He grabs my hands, imploring me to listen. It's too late to argue, I'm too tired and don't care enough to put up a fight. I just nod with a sigh and sit back watching him leave the car and ascend the steps.

The man steps out of the shadows and right up to Rhys, nose to nose they stand under the lamp. Rhys shakes his head coolly and points to the sidewalk, but the man doesn't budge. I see Charlie from the corner of my eye move towards the stoop, but Rhys waves him off and he returns to the car and continues to unload the bags, keeping one eye on Rhys. The man takes a step closer to Rhys invading his space, pushing him back, and Rhys grabs his collar. The man looks towards the car with a sneer on his face before a flash goes off rapid fire and Rhys' stunned face lights up. When the flashing stops, another man emerges from the shadows and takes off running down the street with Charlie hot on his heels. The guy backs away from Rhys with his hands in the air and hops down the steps. I hear Rhys' booming voice call after him, "You motherfucker!" He takes off down the street after the sneak with the camera. Rhys stands under the porch light shaking his head, his hands fisted at his sides, steam rising from his ears. I slide from the car and scurry up the steps into his waiting arms, but the anger etched in his face tells me not to say a word. Not yet.

A deep angry breath shoots from his nose as he wraps his arms around me and turns towards the door. Once inside, he kicks the door closed behind us, steps out of his shoes and walks away from me, leaving me standing at the door in the dark. I see the light go on in his office and hear the door close, and here I stand, in the dark, all alone. I hear a commotion and then the sound of breaking glass, and I stay right where I am. Charlie opens the door behind me, cussing up a storm with my bag dragging behind him. He reaches behind me and flips on the foyer light.

"Christ, Lass, why are ye standing in the dark? Nearly gave me a spell. I'm already clutching my heart from chasing after that fuck."

"Who was that?" I ask after him as he drags my bags up the stairs.

"Sophie!" Rhys' voice booms from within his office before I can get an answer. I freeze for a moment, asking myself if I really want to walk willingly into the lion's den when he is clearly hungry for blood. "Sophie, come in here!" My feet make the decision and take me down the hallway. I stop and take a deep breath of courage before opening the door, expecting to find mayhem, yet finding no such thing.

He sits at his desk, fingers at his lips, his eyes zeroed in on me. There is no anger in his face, perhaps a bit of frustration, but mostly remorse. I look over at the pile of glass in the corner and the busted frame that lies in splinters amongst the shards, and back to him. He just lowers his head and pushes back from his desk.

"Come here, Sophie." I step to him pensively, watching his every move, but he stays still, watching me. I round the desk and he snakes his hand around my hip, sliding me directly in front of him. I lean back against the desk and just wait. He rests his head against my stomach, his hands heavy on my hips.

"Who was that, Rhys?" He shakes his head and pulls himself closer to me. "Rhys," I lift his eyes to mine, making him look at me, "what is going on?"

He shakes me off, refusing to answer. "I fucking love you, Sophie," his raspy whisper tears at me. "You know that, right? I love you and I will not let anybody get in our way. Nobody will take you away from me. Do you understand? Nobody." He rests his hand over my heart. "This is mine," he whispers.

"Yes," I gasp as his hands roam, caressing my breasts, skating down my sides, over the curve of my hips and down over my thighs. His fingertips brand my skin while a dying anger falls from his face. He pushes my skirt up, watching my face with no expression. I focus on him as he pushes his hands higher up my thighs, his fingertips brushing the silken fabric of my panties. A bolt shoots from my pussy, but I stay still, unwilling to betray my emotions or his current mood. I will not react; I will mirror him and be what he needs me to be in this moment. *His*.

"I need to show you, Sophie." He stands up, kicking the chair away from him, lifting me onto the desk. Hooking his fingers in my panties, he tugs at them until I lift myself up. They drop at my feet and he kicks them away, grabbing the hem of my shirt, he whips that away and makes quick work of my bra. And here I sit, my bare ass on his desk, his wild eyes devouring me, making a plan for his hands. He has a cool control over himself in the moment as he steps back and slowly unbuttons his shirt. The crisp cotton slips down his arms, his muscles twisting and turning under tight skin. A slight twitch at his shoulder tells me he is holding back. Unbuckling his belt and undoing the button on his trousers, he steps between my legs, filling the empty void.

"Rhys..." He doesn't allow me to finish the thought. With a nod of his head and a stern look in his eyes, he pushes me to my back, lays his hand open across my chest, and holds me flat on the desk.

"No talking; let me show you." I lay my head against the desk in a sign of surrender. He grabs my ankles and lifts my feet onto the desk, opening me wide to his gaze. My knees fall together instinctively to cover myself from his sight, but he won't allow it. He pushes my knees apart and moves my feet as wide as my hips will allow, toes curled over the edge of the desk. I brace myself, look to the ceiling and just breathe. The crisp night air washes over my exposed pussy and I shiver, not from the cold, but from the anticipation.

He takes his time; his moves calculated and deliberate, running his hands down the inside of my legs all the way to my ankle and slowly back up again. Coming just to the fold of my leg, I can feel the heat from his fingertips, but he won't give it to me. Down the outside of my legs and back up again, he wraps his hands beneath my back and I arch off the desk. His warm breath spreads across my belly and his lips spread slow, soft fire across my skin. Back and forth, he sweeps his mouth across my stretched form, his hands holding me tightly. I feel the velvet of his tongue run from my belly button, leaving a trail of warmth behind until he rests his head between my breasts. He turns his face and presses himself into my chest, taking a deep breath, pulling me deep in his lungs. Craning his neck to the ceiling as he takes a deep breath as if to let gravity pull me deeper. When he looks down on me, he is a man consumed. There is nothing reflected in his eyes, but his hunger for me. He is about to devour me and I am his willing meal.

He devours my pussy with wild abandon, holding me down while he feasts on my flesh. His hot breath sends me flying and his moans make me greedy. I buck off the desk when he wraps his tongue around my clit, but his strong arms don't give an inch.

When I open my eyes, he is standing over me with a carnal twinkle in his eyes. He pushes into me with his fingers, his palm bumping my aching clit with every thrust. A pressure builds so powerful and wrought with need I think I may pass out and he continues to pump my pussy for all its worth. He presses down beneath my belly with his other hand as his fingers thrust upwards and I cry out and crumble. Tremors rack my body and he is relentless, continuing to pummel me while his lips are pulled in a mad grin.

Just as I start to catch my breath, he speeds up and I see stars before I hear an audible crack and I completely let go. Like honey running slowly from

the jar my limbs melt over the desk, my body falls
away and I float high above it all. I couldn't stop if I
wanted to, my body stutters and trembles
uncontrollably, my heart beats in my pussy,
pounding in my head. He pulls his fingers from my
body and sinks back between my fallen legs. He
calms me with his soft lips and brings my clit back
to life with gentle flicks of his tongue before he
pulls me from the desk and into his arms.

I curl up in his lap while he rubs my back and
brings me back to earth.

"I am sorry, Sophie," he strokes my hair while
he quietly laments, "for everything I have put you
through. I hate that anything I have done has hurt
you and you continue to be caught in the crossfire. I
wish I could just make it all stop."

"Are you going to tell me what that was about
tonight? Let me help you, Rhys, don't shut me out."
He squeezes me a bit tighter and sighs.

"You know what it's about, Sophie. What it has
always been about."

"Nadja," I whisper, and his body tenses at the
mention of her name. "Rhys, I love you and I won't
let her drive me away again, I promise."

"I don't know what I've done to deserve you,
Sophie, but I know that I will do everything in my
power to keep you." He kisses the top of my head.

"Well, if you want to keep me, you have to talk
to me. Let me in, whatever it is, we will handle it

together. You can trust me, Rhys." A heavy sigh of relief and trepidation escape his chest before he responds.

"She has a lot of tricks up her sleeve, Sophie, and she is being backed into a corner. I don't even know what to expect next, but I know something is coming. She has never let go easily or walked away quietly and now, with you, she seems positively possessed. The things she has already done have caught me by surprise, her lies and sheer determination to tear us apart is unbelievable. That man tonight was just the tip of the iceberg; she is definitely not done with us."

"Who was he?"

"He is a leech and he wants a story." He takes a deep breath and shifts me in his lap so I can see his face. The pain in his eyes and the set of his jaw tell me I'm in for a ride. "When we were in Ireland, the morning of the phone call, the call was from a reporter, a man I once counted among my friends, but it turns out I was very wrong. All this time while you were figuring out her game, she was changing her moves, Sophie. She has done what I feared the most, what she has always threatened and gone to the press. When we were at Brigid's and he called, he was asking questions about the baby and how I could leave Nadja and flee the country with you. He knew who you were and where we were."

"But that's not your baby, Rhys. We know

this."

"It doesn't matter what we know, Sophie, all that matters is what they print. She has Page Six wrapped around her finger. The fact that he was waiting for us tonight, that he was able to get that picture is proof enough that we are in for a rough ride. There is really no way to combat it. I don't want you exposed to all of this, but it seems she has gone out of her way already to fill the talking heads in on you and her twisted view of our relationship. I don't know that I can protect you, Sophie, and it scares the shit out of me."

I see the fear etched on his face, his eyes full of pain that I know I cannot take away. Powerless to help and clueless as to what is coming next, I remain steadfast, despite my own trepidation. I caress his cheek and muster a sweet smile.

"We protect each other. She has already done her worst to get rid of me, Rhys. I'm a fighter and so are you."

"I have a feeling that things are going to get very ugly, Sophie. It's clear to me that she has abandoned any propriety here. She is operating on sheer malice and she hasn't tapped all her avenues yet. If he was waiting for us tonight there will be a story in the morning, I can guarantee it. She is going to do everything in her power to drag your name through the mud. She wants to tear me down and you with me."

"Rhys, my name means nothing. Let her drag me through the mud, I don't care. I have nothing to prove. I love you. Your opinion is the only one that matters to me."

"You don't know what you're talking about, Sophie. Your name is about family, and family is everything. You have never had to deal with this, never had to see your name and face splattered across newspapers, and never yet had to deal with the snickers and speculation of strangers. Some have the decency to talk behind your back, but many will bring it right to your face. It is brutal and unforgiving and people are rabid for this kind of gossip. She is going to use every resource at her disposal to try and humiliate me, and worse, to humiliate you." His pulse rate visibly spikes, given away by the angry vein throbbing in his neck. He shifts me from his lap and stands, pacing like a wild animal. I gather my clothes and watch him closely as his anger blooms and he mutters to himself under his breath. He stops and shakes his head, his eyes wild, his breathing heavy. When he turns back to me there is a twisted determination on his face.

"I am going to fucking destroy her." The quiet antipathy in his voice sends a chill down my spine and the hate in his eyes flares when he looks at me. "Two can play this game. If she wants a war, who am I to deny her? My pockets are deeper than her bench. I'll take her down and everyone else with her if that's what she wants."

"That's not who you are," I whisper.

"You don't know who I am," he lashes out and stings me, pacing, wearing a trail across the floor. Anger rolls off his back and I am struck by that fact that I have never seen this man, this anger.

"Rhys, this isn't you, please, I've never seen you like this. Think about what you are doing."

"You don't know shit about me. You know what I want you to know." The words cut deep and my spine rattles from the blow. I shudder under the weight of his growing fury and icy cold tone. His face is twisted in pain and anger. He stalks across the room like a rabid beast, unpredictable and volatile.

"I know that you are better than what she has reduced you to. I know that you don't want to punish other people for what she has done." He stops pacing and zeroes in on me.

"Why are you defending her?"

"I am not defending her. I am defending you. You are Rhys fucking Slate, you are powerful and shrewd. You could buy and sell her, but you are letting her push you off the rails again. She is in your head. You are blinded by your rage and she is winning. Every moment you spend thinking about her, she gets what she wants. Don't give her the satisfaction."

"I'm so sorry, Sophie, I just don't know how to

deal with her anymore. All she responds to is extremes. I cannot, and will not, allow her to hurt you one more time. I do not know what to do." His shoulders sag and he falls back into his chair, head in his hands. He looks so broken, his stony façade crumbling before me all because of this vindictive bitch and her lies.

"Trust me." I step between his legs and rest my hands on his shoulders. "Together, we can handle this."

"I wish I had your confidence," he pulls me into his lap and holds me tight, "your blind confidence."

"Sometimes being blind allows you to see things more clearly."

"Aren't you wise?" He smiles and I see the cracks in his anger spread. "We will face tomorrow together."

CH. 17

I slept like a log and when I finally wake I am alone and the sun is high. I find Rhys and Charlie in the kitchen, Rhys on his laptop, Charlie flipping through a Sports Illustrated. Rhys looks up with a wink and pushes a newspaper towards me.

"Together." The paper is folded open to Page Six and sure enough, there she is in all her lying glory; made for the society page, leaving some restaurant with an entourage. But it's the headline that really catches my attention.

Lady and the Tramp
You're Not in Kansas Anymore

There's a picture of me coming out of Rhys' office building, completely unaware, my name printed in big bold letters just beneath. I make the mistake of reading on…

Longtime lovers and media darlings Rhys Slate and Nadja Vladova have come up against their most formidable foe to date. It seems the affections of Mr. Slate have been captured by a dowdy Midwest mystery. Rhys Slate, CEO of the Slate Corp., and active board member of several charitable foundations, seems to be slumming it with this unemployed, unremarkable flavor of the month. It seems in recent weeks, Mr. Slate has been MIA,

having run away to Ireland with his little apple tart.
In the weeks he was gallivanting over emerald hills,
Ms. Vladova was reportedly spotted with bruising
on her face and arms, rumored to be the lasting
marks of Mr. Slates well documented anger issues.
Other reports suggest that she is carrying his child,
which is what sparked his anger to begin with.
There was a time when I looked forward to the
reunion of this once epic couple, but in the wake of
recent events, and the ongoing pattern of violence
and humiliation demonstrated by Mr. Slate it seems
all hope for a happy ending is lost. This poor beauty
is lucky to finally be rid of her beast.

Below the scathing editorial is Rhys in black
and white, grabbing that man by the collar last
night, his fist seemingly cocked for a punch. An
unfortunate moment caught out of context.

Angry tears begin to cloud my eyes and I don't
dare look at either of them. I stare at the counter and
fight it, not brave enough to read another word of
the bile splashed across the page. Rhys turns me
around, tipping my head to meet his eyes, betraying
my evident devastation.

"I told you this was going to be hard,
Beautiful." He pulls me into a bear hug, trying to
eclipse the pain but the cut is too deep.

For two days I feign a headache, not wanting to
leave the house or face the outside world. He sees

right through me, but caters to me none the less, sending Charlie out for soup and cupcakes. Come Sunday morning he will no longer be put off and insists that we walk around the corner for breakfast.

"It's just a block away Sophie. I won't be held hostage and I won't let you hide away. I want to walk hand in hand and have some damn pancakes, is that too much to ask?" I catch myself sweeping the street with my eyes, back and forth as we walk down the block and around the corner, weary of anyone passing. Charlie hangs two paces back until we reach the restaurant.

"See, Beautiful, we made it unscathed and I'm famished. We are yesterday's news." A quick kiss as Charlie opens the door and we step into the busy little diner. At the end of the counter a waitress stands with her hand in the air.

"We've got three at the end!" She hollers over the morning chatter, pointing to the end of the counter. I follow behind Charlie, sandwiched between him and Rhys. We sidle up to the last three stools at the counter. "Coffee, hun?"

I pick my way through half an order of French toast while Charlie glances nervously out the window. Rhys pushes his omelet around the plate, always watching over the top of his coffee cup. The crowd is growing and there is a line forming on the sidewalk as well, all normal for a Saturday breakfast rush, but it's the hushed whispers and sideways glances that are the deciding factor.

"Come Sophie, finish up, let's go before it gets too crowded." I look up and see the shadow across Charlie's face and Rhys tapping his fingers on his coffee mug.

We quickly finish and Rhys leaves far too much money on the counter, but he is in a hurry. Charlie gets in front of me and Rhys walks behind as we make our way through the growing crowd of waiting hungry patrons. I feel his hand at my back and stay close to Charlie. When he pushes the door open I am blinded first by sunlight, then by flash bulbs. In an instant I hear yelling erupt.

"Mr. Slate, Mr. Slate!" Rhys pushes me from behind, but someone grabs my arm and pulls me away. I reach out and try to grab Charlie, but he has been pushed in the opposite direction, out of my reach. Rhys is surrounded by a throng of men with cameras, shouting his name, throwing accusations in the air, hoping something will provoke him.

"Rhys! Do you have a comment about your relationship with Nadja?" I hear him call my name but I can't see him through the crowd.

"Do you have a comment about the miscarriage?" The words carry over everything, *the miscarriage*.

I see Charlie throw a punch and push some guy down to the sidewalk. There's a camera in my face, snap, snap, snap. The photographer documents my fear and confusion wearing an odd grin.

"Welcome to New York!" His smile is temporary as Charlie lunges towards me and grabs my hand, knocking the man out of the way, pulling me through a small crowd of people. He wraps his arms around my shoulders, pushing my gaze to the ground, and leads me away from the mayhem.

"Keep your head down, Lass." He drags me along the sidewalk, away from Rhys, away from the yells. When we turn the corner, he turns to me, tilts my head to his and checks me over. "Are ya okay, Sophie? Are ya hurt?"

I just shake my head, no confidence in my voice.

"Rhys." I whisper.

"He will be fine, he will meet us at home. Let's get moving before those leeches come looking for ya. Hustle now." He grabs my hand and pulls me along the street.

CH. 18

I sit at the edge of the bed in shock, terrified and feeling completely over my head, questioning my ability to deal with this spiraling situation. Charlie paces behind me professing his regret, however misplaced. I can't believe how swiftly I was swept away from him, separated by a wave of people, isolated and intimidated. I've never experienced a fear like that, the sheer terror of having absolutely no control. My heart races at the echo of their yells. I focus on a point across the room and take a deep breath in an attempt to center myself.

Rhys sweeps into the room looking slightly winded, but otherwise unscathed. He and Charlie share a few quiet words before Charlie steps out, closing the door behind him.

"Are you ok, Beautiful" He kneels before me, sweeping the hair behind my ears, running his hands up my arms, no doubt looking for scrapes and bruises. And though there is none to be seen, the scrapes to my ego are bleeding. I look into his eyes, unable to process, unable to focus.

"Talk to me, Sophie. Tell me you are ok." A mumbled response escapes my lips, but my head is still reeling. I have never seen anything like that, never experienced such in your face aggression. I was torn away from him so easily.

"I don't know what happened, Rhys. All of a sudden I was alone. I couldn't see you, but I could hear you. It was fucking scary. I felt so lost." I hang my head in shame.

"I am so sorry, Sophie. I will never let that happen again." He reaches up and kisses me with the force of the universe behind him and I fall headlong into him. He wraps his arms around me and pulls me close and I can breathe again. Even as he pulls the very breath from my mouth I can breathe. "In a sea of people I will always find you, Beautiful." He is out of breath and desperate, kissing me with such beautiful words in his mouth.

"I was missing something before you, something essential. You are that something. You have become a part of me Sophie, the best part." He bites my bottom lip, pulling it slowly through his teeth before soothing it with his tongue. His hands are tangled in my hair and I claw at his back unable to get close enough. He pushes me back and scans me with his eyes.

I feel completely transparent and weak. The way his eyes rake me over, slowly reading my body. My skin like a delicate piece of vellum lies over an open book, every private thought scrawled across the pages for him to read. I am laid open to him, unable to hide myself, and I relish the exposure. I want him to drink me in, as I have done; to read every word that I cannot say, to see the indelible finger prints he has left upon my flesh and my soul.

"You own me, Sophie, my heart beats for you, but I need you to talk to me, to let me in. Let me take care of you, show you that you are safe." He produces a pair of suede cuffs and slaps them onto my wrists. I look up into his mischievous eyes, searching for something.

"Let me take your mind away, away from all of this. Let me show you." I don't have it in me to deny him anything, I will endure the lot for this man. To have him kneeling at my feet, desperate to prove his love and offer his protection is intoxicating and I want it all now. I need him, so I let him. He stands and undoes his belt. The slide of the leather through his belt loops makes my mouth water. Pulling it across his open palm he nods at me.

"Take off your shirt, Sophie.' I whip my shirt over my head and drop it swiftly to the floor, releasing my bra eagerly and in the next moment, letting it slide down my arms. A slight grin raises his mouth and he silently demands my hands. I lay my wrists out for him and watch with baited breath, lust pulsing through my veins as he wraps my wrists in the supple leather of his belt and pulls it tight.

"Turn around and lie down, Beautiful, hands above your head. I roll over and lay my face on the bed, wiping my tears on the duvet, stretching my arms high above me. His hands skate across my back, tracing my spine, laying their claim to my strength. He climbs on the bed, kneeling behind me and places his hands at my hips, pulling me to my knees. "Bottoms up," he purrs. My back is arched, ass to the sky with my arms stretched out. A tiny tremble rolls across my hips when I feel his fingers hook into my shorts, slowly pulling them and my panties down around my knees, he sits back on his heels, making a meal out of watching me squirm.

"Up on your elbows baby." A master of disarmament, I am no match with a belt around my wrists and anchored to the spot. I look around to see what he has planned, but he snaps, "Eyes on the wall."

Turning back to the wall, I close my eyes in anticipation. The waiting is agony as he teases me, his hands skating lusciously up and down my back and legs from neck to toe. Over and over, the rhythm is hypnotic. I am lost to it, consumed by his hands, by his scent, by his intent. He splays his fingers across my back, pulling them down my spine, across my buttocks and down the back of my thighs. The sensation ripples through me and I shudder slightly before I am snapped back by the feeling of his tongue.

His hands grip the back of my thighs as he slowly runs his tongue along my seam. I sag, but his hands hold me fast. His tongue runs up and down, pressing just beyond the cheeks, each time wetting and teasing neglected, wanting flesh. I am awake to a whole new world as he teases and strokes me, exploring my deepest recess. He rests a heavy hand on my back and begins to circle my clit. The tight, achy bunch of nerves spring into action, a ripple rolling down to my knees causing them to shake.

"You have yet to talk Sophie. Tell me what you want, what you need, what you're afraid of." This is not good. If there is anything that I have learned about Rhys in the short time we have known each other is that he does not give up. He wants something from me and he is going to get it. Whatever it is.

I hear him slide back and slip off his pants before he is behind me again, his fingers digging slightly into my hips. He lies across my back and whispers in my ear, "I cannot have you keeping things from me, Sophie. You allow so much to go unsaid."

A small involuntary moan escapes my throat as his hips push against me, the anticipation building to a head, my body ready to explode, but I say nothing. He places a hand at the base of my throat; it is erotic and a little scary. I feel his hand push against my chest as his cock slips inside of me; he is buried to the hilt and still. The fullness and mere contact are almost enough to pull me under. I pulse around him, pulling him deeper, begging him to move. He starts to push into me and pull out, slowly at first, shallow thrusts, gentle pressure and desperate pleas in a hushed whisper. Before I know it, he is slamming into me. His body rigid, his knuckles white from the grip he has on my hips, pulling me onto him, pushing me off. He is emotional, uncontrolled, and raw.

"Why won't you talk to me? What is holding you back?" He slams into me mercilessly, trying to force me to confess. I am hot and sexed, confused and angry. His fingers dig into my hips and he lies across my back. The contact is heavy, his sticky skin coating my back with the proof of his virility. He lays his lips against my shoulder and kisses me softly. Slowing his hips, he strains against his own urges. His hot breath slides across my ear, sending a shiver down my spine. "You really need to tell me what is holding you back…" The delicate kiss he places between my shoulder blades is no warning. He rises up and slams into me with such ferocity that my arms buckle, I sink to my elbows and press back against him. I know he means to punish me, to fuck me into submission, but all he has done is wake a sleeping beast. Every deep thrust is proof, the proof that I need proof that he needs me as much as I need him. I rock my hips against him and he stills.

"Oh no, Sophie. This is not for you." He flips me around and pulls my hips to the edge of the bed. My arms stretched high above me, the edge of the leather biting the soft flesh of my hands.

"You will tell me what is holding you back."

His head dips between my legs and he takes a long, heady breath, his blazing eyes focused so intently on my reaction to his brazen sexual attack. I want to look away, but he won't let me. "Watch me," he demands. He softly spreads me open and blows a steady stream of cool air over me. I am hot and wet, well used with no end in sight. He grins that crooked grin and slowly presses a finger past my puffy folds. Twisting and turning, he slides his finger to the knuckle before pulling back. He puts the finger to his lips and slowly sucks it into his mouth. "Mmm," he moans, licking every drop of me from his finger. My eyes roll and I let my head fall back.

"Watch me," he growls, demanding my attention. My head is so heavy; my body limp from the relentless onslaught. I manage to drag my head up and his eyes are on fire when they meet mine. If he wasn't making me feel so good I would swear he was trying to kill me. With his eyes locked on mine, he flicks my flesh, carefully kissing every tender, swollen inch before spearing me with his tongue. The sensation is overwhelming and rocks me to my core. A lightning bolt runs through me and I am ready to ride it home, but Rhys has other plans. He rolls back onto his heels, leaving me empty. Hands firmly planted on his thighs, watching me impassively as the orgasm dies and my face falls. It is almost painful, the dull ache of so much pent up energy trapped just below the surface, searing me from within, screaming to be released.

He slides back between my legs, starting the process all over; pressing his fingers into me, swirling and stretching me open, blowing his hot breath on my inflamed lips. His tongue dips in and out, twisting around my clit teasing and torturing me. With each small tremor, he sits back and watches me burn, waiting for me to beg. The ache in my belly has grown to a dull roar. I can't stand it. I have to come now and hard. I am afraid of what my body will do when he finally lets me uncurl.

"What do you want? Please, Rhys. I cannot take another minute." My voice shakes in unison with my legs, hot tears stream down my face. I am spent, needy and broken. His strong arms anchor my legs; his eyes have me tied down, expectant, and waiting.

"What do I have to do to make you understand?" He slowly presses a second finger into the raging inferno between my legs. The contact is slow, delicious and utterly painful. Before he can push any further, I crack.

"I'm afraid!" I scream at him. "I'm afraid that I can't handle this, that you'll tire of taking care of me. I have so little to offer you! I don't want to lose you; I would be lost. Please, Rhys." He slowly climbs over me, softly lapping the tears from my jaw. He strokes my cheek with the back of his hand.

He is calm, tender, and starkly different from a moment ago. He gazes into my eyes and the flood gates open. "You have everything. I have nothing of value. Nothing you need."

His hands cup my face, eyes wide with shock. "I need you, Sophie." My arms feel like lead as I raise them from the bed and slip my bound wrists over his head. He sits up and pulls me into his lap and in two easy movements undoes the belt and begins to unwind it from my wrists. My arms pulse and throb and I flex my hands as the blood rushes into my fingertips. I blink up at him through a curtain of tears, and he looks lost, broken. "I'm sorry, Sophie." His fingers slide down my arms, checking me over. Curled against his chest I feel safe, but I ache. From the deepest part of me the ache rises like smoke.

"Why? Why do you need me?" His hands are in my hair, caressing and comforting. All traces of his ferocious sexual taming evaporated the instant I confessed; a confession I had not planned, a confession that caught me by surprise.

"I don't understand." His hands are in my hair, caressing and comforting. All traces of his ferocious sexual taming evaporated the instant I confessed. A confession I had not planned, a confession that caught me by surprise.

"I will make you understand," he insists, "what do I have to do?"

"Finish what you started," I beg.

I watch him quickly change character and sink back in amongst the pillows and soft down. He covers me with his body, careful not to crush my aching form. Yet, the weight of him upon me is anything but oppressive. It is a relief. Something deep inside me needs the weight he has come to bear. Brushing the hair off my forehead, he kisses my lips, softly first, and then with an urgency that builds so quickly between us the air grows heavy and hot. He wraps his arms around me and before I know it, I am astride him and he is beneath me.

He grasps my hands and holds me aloft for a sweet, delicate moment before he bucks his hips and sends me into the air. I ride him like my life depends on it, like the tip of his cock holds the secret to life and I am the deepest cave; all of our secrets hidden in its depths that only we can reach. My body happily pillaged by his demanding lust, a sticky sheen the proof of our shared desperation. He labors to possess me and I give him no choice but to accept my surrender.

He pulls me down against him, skin to skin, my breasts crushed against his rigid chest. Our hearts beat like bass drums answering back and forth, blood surging through my body and him whispering in my ear.

"This pussy is mine, this body is mine, and I will remind you when you forget," his rough whisper rattles in my ear. "This pussy is mine, this body is mine, your heart is fucking mine." He chants, getting louder, squeezing me closer, "This pussy is mine, this body is mine, this heart is mine." He sinks his teeth into my shoulder as I roll myself against him, the heat between us burning me up, making me so fucking needy. He holds me still, his strong arms wrapped around me like a strait jacket, growling in my ear. He tears me apart with a brutal thrust that sends my eyes rolling back in my head. "This pussy is mine, Beautiful. Your body is mine; your heart is fucking mine. You. Are. Mine," he pants, "and I am yours."

"Yes," I mumble, barely coherent as our bodies slow and he loosens his grip. But he doesn't leave me, we settle into each other and find a slow rhythm as he rocks his hips and I crest his rolling cock. It's like love in slow motion as I rise and fall on the pillar of this man who now owns my body the way he has owned my heart. He rests his hands on my hips and watches me, and I just can't help myself. My hands roam over my sticky skin up and over the curve of my bouncing breasts. I cup one; the heft is remarkable when I feel so light. I pinch and twist my nipple between my fingers and watch his eyes light up. A coy smile takes my mouth as the other hand travels south to the point where we meet. I look him in the eye and start circling my clit, focused on the sensation, slow and deliberate, matching his measured thrusts. Flames glimmer behind his eyes and it's evident he is on the verge of losing control. His fingers dig deeper into my flesh and he guides my body, moving me up and down his slick shaft, circling his hips to hit that sweet spot that makes me whimper with delight.

"Come for me, Sophie," he quietly demands, "do it now." He locks his eyes on me, "now." His voice propels me and within the blink of an eye, I press down on my throbbing clit and release a world of emotion. The ecstasy is almost too much, it wells up in my throat and erupts as a cry before turning into the most satisfying, soul rattling moan to ever escape my throat. My head falls forward, every joint in my body limp, no longer able to fight off the aftershocks that rock my bones and steal my breath.

He holds me aloft and thrusts his cock deeper as I come around him, each thrust prolonging my little death as he builds ever closer to his own. The moment of impact is oddly quiet but deeply profound as I'm sure the earth moved and we stood still. Our eyes locked, our bodies united, our hearts beat as one. I am out of breath, out of steam, and out of fight. There is no going back. I am his and he is mine. There is nothing else.

CH. 19

Early Monday morning and I pace like a wildcat wearing a path in the floor, back and forth in front of the window, watching the early morning traffic, watching the door, waiting for the phone to ring, thinking about Sophie twisted up in my sheets. When Nina finally buzzes, the silence has almost sucked the oxygen from the room.

I watch her walk down the hall towards my office and swear every pane of glass fogs over like she's bringing a chill with her. Her face is lit up, her smile demure and practiced. She looks wholly confident just as I knew she would. *Play on her vanity.*

I open the door for her and she lowers her eyes when we come face to face before slowly stepping around me and lowering herself into the chair before my desk, never quite looking me in the eye.

"You'll have to forgive me, I am still recovering. I've been through quite bit the last few months." Her voice is quiet, pensive.

"And I'm sorry for it," I say, rounding my desk. "I've read that you have been through quite an ordeal." She looks up at me, shooting daggers from her dark eyes. "How is Sergei?" I take a seat, watching her every move. She barely raises an eyebrow in reaction before shrugging it off coolly.

"I haven't seen the man in months." She throws the coat off of her shoulders and sits forward in her chair; picking up a framed picture sitting on my desk, a picture of me and my father. She looks it over with a smirk before replacing it, meeting my eyes in defiance. "What is this all about?"

"I've asked you here to call a truce; to offer you your just desserts, whatever you want it's yours, name your price. We both know what is real and what is not here, but I am willing to let it all go and just move on, if you are willing to do the same."

"No," she returns flatly, never looking away. "I have no idea what you are implying, but surely whatever has been happening to you is something you reaped. You should watch how you treat people, Rhys." She cocks her head and her lips twist in a snide grin. 'No, I think I have earned my time and I am going to enjoy this. Now, if you'd like me to lay off your little toy all you have to do is get rid of her. It's as easy as that."

"I'm not ever going to do that, Nadja. I love Sophie, she is here to stay.

"You said anything I want."

"Yes, within reason."

"I don't see what is unreasonable about wanting her gone. I lost something I love. Turnabout is fair play."

"Indeed."

"Well, I won't be replaced by her, Rhys. I won't have her coming in and taking my place. You can't just replace me, certainly not with someone like her." The quiet malice in her voice is mesmerizing. Her calm masks a slowly erupting body, her hands slightly trembling as she scoots to the edge of her chair. "Do not underestimate me, Rhys, I am nowhere near done. You have humiliated me and I plan to return the favor." She stands and grabs her coat. This is spiraling out of control quickly, she can't leave yet.

I center myself and calmly take the coat from her trembling hands.

"When were you going to tell me about the baby?' I soften my gaze and lower my voice. Her eyes grow wide before she steps nose to nose with me.

"Why would I tell you? You wouldn't care."

"The baby was not mine, Nadja. If ever there was a baby to begin with," my voice even and calm.

"You don't know what you are talking about," her voice cracking as her hand goes to her belly, but she stops herself.

"The baby was not mine." I push her back into her seat with a cold stare, struggling not to react to her. There used to be love there in her eyes, in my eyes, I'm sure, but that love has been poisoned by both of us. There is pain in her eyes for a split second when she looks at me, but it's promptly replaced with revulsion.

"Prove it," she slowly replies, resolved not to

crumble.

"I am sorry." A silence falls over the room as she and I both absorb the shocking sincerity of my apology. She sits back in her chair and takes a breath.

"What are you sorry for?"

"Sorry for all the hurt I have caused you. I'm sorry for what you are going through. I am sorry for what has happened to us." She opens her mouth to respond and quickly shuts it, her brow wrinkles in confusion; hearing me apologize so convincingly to her makes my skin crawl.

"I am sorry, Nadja. Truly." She sits back and waits for more. "But, hurting me, hurting Sophie, will not make your pain go away. It won't make anything go away."

Like a changeling, she morphs the instant my words register.

"Perhaps," she returns coolly, "but it will make me feel better." She smiles, waiting for a response. I don't give in, rounding my desk confidently quiet, shoulders set, mouth slightly turned, knowing that I've got her right where I want her. I lower myself to my chair, eyes fixed on Nadja as she fiddles with her coat. "I do hope this meeting's sole purpose was not to chastise me, Rhys." She shifts, facing me head on, her long legs stretched in front of her, crossed at the ankle.

"This is, after all, my year. Is it not? It was me

that brought in the most money this past year, it is my programs that brought the most press. The Blue Ball is about me this year." She tosses her hair and glances up at me coyly, "Why aren't we talking about that?"

"Alright, Nadja, we can talk about that."

"I worked hard for this honor, Rhys, and I would like to enjoy it," she sits back and splays her fingers across the arms of the chair calmly, "with you, the way people expect, the way it should be."

"Nadja," I sit forward, resting my elbows on the desk, "I don't believe that people expect to see us together. Not after the damage you have caused."

"I did not cause all that damage alone, Rhys, but together we can fix it. All it will take is one good picture, one good blurb, you know how it works, and all of this can go away."

"Right," I respond slowly, sitting back in my chair, "you are going to make all of this go away."

CH 20

I watch him get ready, work a little pomade in his hair to tame those curls I love so much. A meticulous shave that leaves him rugged but polished. Perfection all the way down to his feet, the towel barely hanging on to his hips like a tease.

I watch her get ready, dab her cheeks with lotion, and spray her skin with my favorite perfume. Her hair wildly whipping about as she blows it dry. She glances over and catches me watching, that beautiful bubble gum flush catching her freckles on fire.

Sliding his arms into his dress shirt he watches me cross the room.

She slinks into the closet and drops her towel unaware of my eyes.

I walk into the closet and drop my towel, well aware that he is watching me. As I bend to step into my new silk panties his hands snake around my hips and I feel his swell against my ass. I stand and he whispers hotly in my ear.

"Are you trying to drive me mad?" She smiles coyly, pressing back against me, that sexy hum rolling down her throat. I grab her by the jaw and turn her to face me, a delighted smirk across her face.

"Is it working?" I tease as he holds my attention firmly in his hand. He just smiles before taking my mouth in his and sucking the sass right

out of me. He sweeps my legs off the ground lifting me onto the dresser.

I push her legs open and pull her hips to the edge. I need to fuck her now and I need to fuck her hard. She reaches to kiss me and I speak the directive into her mouth. "Hold on to me, love."

I wrap my arms beneath the collar of his open shirt and hold on tight as he thrusts his cock into me without any ceremony or pomp. He pulls back and does it again, pushing himself to the hilt, our hips crushed together. An animalistic groan starts low in his throat as he pulls back and drives into me over and over. He wraps his hand behind my neck and pulls me forward resting his forehead against mine. Our eyes lock and he fucks me hard, never looking away. I am hypnotized by his eyes, by his movements and my body hums in electric delight.

I watch her take every inch of me over and over, so wet she must have been waiting for me. Her eyes flare in delight each time I hit that spot and her pussy starts to quiver.

"Come for me, Sophie." I whisper before diving so deep inside her she could never escape. The color drains from her face before her eyes shut and the most melodious moan rises from her throat like smoke on the water. That sound is the death of me and in the next press I lose my focus and come hot and hard into her erupting body. She grips me and pulls me in further, pulsing around me, claiming me as I have claimed her. My mind is wiped clean of anything but us as the evidence of her lust trickles down my leg. Her limp body doesn't cease to shake when I slip my cock from within her, resting her back on the dresser, her legs still tight around my waist.

He is sex on a stick standing before me in his now wrinkled dress shirt and nothing else, his cock bobbing freely still glistening with my cum.

"You should change your shirt." I giggle as he pulls me into a soft kiss.

"Not a chance Beautiful. This way I can smell you all night long." I wrinkle my nose but secretly love the idea of him wearing me all over him, all night long. Especially considering I won't be on his arm as I should be.

He straightens his shirt and I button it for him, taking my time to touch every inch of his chest as I do. I fasten his cuff links and pull his bowtie around his neck before he helps me from the dresser. I decide that I want to wear Rhys all night as well and just straighten my hair before he helps me into the dress Olivia has so graciously loaned me. Deep blue taffeta that she had worn to the same event a few years earlier. I add a lighter blue petticoat under the full circle skirt and a vintage broach to make it my own. He zips the back slowly before sweeping my hair out of the way, pressing his lips to the nape of my neck.

"You look beautiful, Sophie. You are ready for this." I drop my eyes but he won't allow the self-doubt to creep back in. He tips my chin back up, his eyes intent and serious. "You are ready for this." He nods and I nod back.

"Yes." I reply

"Louder Sophie, make me believe it. You need to believe it. Louder."

"Yes, I am ready for this," and as the words come steady and strong I know he is right. He believes in me; I believe in me. I am ready for this.

"Yes my love, you are. This is the beginning for us. Tonight is the first night of the rest of our lives. Together we go forward."

His car arrives just as Olivia and Matthew pull up with Michael. He says a quick goodbye to me on the stoop before bending Matthew and Michael's ear at the car. Olivia looks amazing in a Tiffany blue chiffon gown with a crystal belt around her tiny waist. She hooks her arm into mine and we head into the kitchen.

"You look perfect Sophie," She says inspecting me closely. "That dress is so much cuter on you than it was on me. Well done." She sighs heavily, in that very dramatic Olivia fashion, sitting back on a bar stool. Something is hiding behind her eyes, as if she fights back a knowing smile. I grab a bottle of red wine from the rack and two glasses and hope for some distracting gossip.

"No thanks Sophie. No wine for me." She grins. Before I can form the question I already know the answer.

"Olivia…" She watches my coyly.

"Yep," she replies, "Its official, the rhythm method doesn't work."

"Oh my god!" I squeal and throw my arms around her before quickly remembering our conversation. "Wait, honey, are you ok with this?"

"Yes!" She exclaims, "Yes, Sophie. I am so happy. I don't know what it is, what happens, but the moment I found out for sure I just knew that this is what I wanted. I told you, if it happened it happened and well….it happened." We hug each other and sway like girls do while she tells me how elated Matthew is to be a father and how she plans to keep the news from his mother, just a for a few days, just to see her squirm.

When we finally come up for air from baby talk Michael is standing at the door calling us to the car. He is every inch the gentleman and the spitting image of a more mature Rhys. His wavy silver hair a stunning contrast to his dark blue suit, his bow tie tight and straight. His lips curl in that Slate family grin, those dimples making me melt. We file into o the back of the car and off we go. Into the future, the first night of the rest of our lives, together.

CH. 21

I watch from the back of the Town Car as we crawl down the street, one in a long line of limos and luxury cars. As soon as their door is opened, the flash bulbs start and I see him step from the car and offer his hand. She slips a leg out in grand fashion before slowly rising from the back seat, grasping Rhys' hand and basking in the attention. The slightest flash of jealousy stings before I settle back and remind myself that her glory will be short lived.

I close my eyes and picture Rhys holding my hand, his warm fingers laced with mine, my pulse slows and I am able to take a deeper breath and focus.

She shines in the face of the press, working the carpet, always posing. Her blue lace dress fits like a glove, a delicate pattern poured over her like a second skin. Rhys' dark suit shimmers like a midnight lake in the face of the flashes. I see him look in our direction, knowing he is looking for us. Charlie flashes the lights at him and we slowly crawl to the head of the line as I watch them make their way up the carpet.

Olivia watches me trying so hard not to react as Michael reaches over and takes my hand.

"All will be well, my dear. Big things are in store for you and Rhys, I'm quite sure of that. Don't worry about a thing, it's all in order, you just need to breathe and be as charming as you always are."

He places a fatherly kiss to the back of my hand as the door opens. "Now, it's been quite a while since I have had someone so young and beautiful on my arm. Come and make me look good," he grins helping me from the car.

Michael doesn't stop for the photographers nor does he acknowledge most of the press, but just walks casually by as if they aren't even there. "I generally prefer to avoid the riffraff," he whispers to me as we pass a local television news crew setting up. Olivia and Matthew are a few paces behind us stopping for pictures.

"Gossip is not conducive to business and I for one have never liked big wet noses poking around in my life. This is a new phenomenon here, and I can thank my son for it. It's both a blessing and a curse as you've come to know. But it's always important to be guarded, my dear. Trust should not be easily given, nor should detail."

***

She grabs my arm and pulls me closer.

"Smile, Rhys, everyone is watching," she whispers as she flashes that model smile at the two dozen photographers vying for her attention. I slip on a jovial smile and wrap my arm around her waist, playing the part of a doting escort.

We have cocktails in the lobby and chat up the

few reporters who managed to snag a coveted ticket. Ever since my grandfather started this foundation sixty-five years ago, it has thrived and the Blue Ball has always been the crowning event where top donators are celebrated, new connections and avenues are forged, and upcoming projects are revealed. The apex of our year and this year will be no exception, I've made sure Sophie will never forget it, nor will I.

Inside the ballroom elegant tables dot the well-appointed room, crystal chandeliers drip from the high arched ceiling, candles flicker by the dozens on each table and the stage is set for the chamber orchestra and band. A quartet sits in the corner and plays softly as the crowd files in with their champagne flutes, being led off in every direction by an army of ushers showing them all to their tables.

We mingle and wait for most to be seated before I walk Nadja to the largest table perched at the edge of the dance floor and adjacent to the stage. As I pull out her chair, the emcee takes the stage and opens the evening.

I scan the room for Sophie, knowing full well she is with my father and he never partakes in the meal, preferring instead to stay in the lobby and give a chosen reporter a few exclusives on upcoming projects or future endowments.

He has always been more comfortable among

them than I and I've always been thankful for that, but I wonder how Sophie is faring among them. I wish she was next to me instead of insipid Nadja with her smug grin. I watch her push her salad around her plate, feigning interest in what is being discussed at the table. She looks up at me and rolls her eyes before pouring half a glass of champagne down her throat, careful not to smudge her blood red lips.

***

We pass the marble lions that guard the door into the theater. The lobby drips with crystal chandeliers and white silk banners, and goddesses dressed in white serving cocktails and ushering guests to the ballroom. Michael and I circle the room before he leads me to the bar.

"I like to make a round and then have a round" His green eyes twinkle and his dimple shows when he winks, motioning for the bartender. "What would you like, Sophie?"

"I'll have whatever you're having." His approving smile makes me oddly proud, but I also know that I need a stiff drink. A glass of wine will not tame these nerves. To my left and right, I am surrounded by eye candy dripping with diamonds, power and influence wrapped in designer tuxedos. Everybody is somebody.

"The Balvenie, please, two fingers, neat." The crowd funnels into the dining room, leaving a handful of discreetly operating members of the press who lack the appropriate ticket or net worth to go any further. Several men seem to be conducting a business deal much to their companion's chagrin, as well as the staff's. Michael raises his glass to me, "To new beginnings and family."

"Cheers." I take a slow, measured sip tasting honey and caramel as the scotch coats my tongue like velvet. Michael takes a hearty pull before waving over a gentleman from the corner. He is older than the rest, noticeably, but wears a press badge and carries the same tools of the trade; a camera around his neck and a smart phone in his hand.

"Mr. Slate, so nice to see you this evening." They shake hands like old friends. "I hear we are in store for a bit of a shake up tonight? Do you care to comment on that?"

"Now, Bernie, you know that I don't. But, I'd like to buy you a drink and introduce you to Sophie here." He places his hand at the small of my back, nudging me into the spotlight. "Sophie, this here is Bernie. He's a financial columnist for the Times and an occasional thorn in my side. Bernie, this is Sophie, my date." He pulls me close with a wink and I go with it. Bernie looks skeptical, but launches into his question without much hesitation.

"I've seen your third quarter numbers, Mr. Slate."

"Please, Bernie, we are having a drink. It's a nice evening, call me Michael, for God's sake and relax will you?" He tips his glass, urging Bernie to partake. He lifts the glass to his lips with a grimace and takes too large of a swig before coughing like an amateur.

CH 22

Waiters filter into the room and circle the tables. Soft music fills the hall while the guests eat and drink and schmooze until the band leader stands and taps his stand, commanding the room's attention. The music swells as the last guests take their seats. When everyone is settled, the lights go down and the spotlight illuminates a small circle on the stage in which The Mayor steps. Applause fills the space before he opens the evening's ceremonies with a predictable joke and a burst of canned laughter. A second spotlight illuminates our table when he introduces first the foundation and then me as the keynote speaker. Nadja predictably slides into the light and kisses me on the cheek, unable to avoid the spotlight even for a moment. She squeezes my hand as I stand and ascend the steps.

"We come together tonight to celebrate a triumphant year, or more accurately a triumphant half century. But as we all know there is always more to be done and we have some big new plans on the horizon.

We have been blessed to watch these amazing children here tonight sharing their hard earned talents. The district wide music program just one of dozens that our team has been responsible for over the years. I know we all agree that music is vital to a growing child's development.

These programs are a partnership between

community and the wonderful artists who donate their time and energy and sharing their passions with these children, who we hope one day, will go and share their passions as well. Giving is a cycle; it's something we simply all must do. In order to build the kind of world that we want for our children, we have to make the world that way for all children."

I look up from my notes and scan the room quickly for any sign of my father or Sophie. At the back of the room, she stands, her arm laced through his, shrouded in shadows yet radiant, she tips her glass with a smile and I continue as she takes her drink.

"We announce two new projects this evening. These are brand new endeavors for our foundation and an exciting twist in our structure.

We have partnered with a group of parents in the Gramercy neighborhood to form a charter school. The Slate Family Foundation and the newly formed PTO will rebuild the recently closed PS 138. The building will be upgraded throughout and the school will triple its size, being able to accommodate the neighborhood children comfortably and with all the necessary technology and advancements that they require

I am very proud of this new direction, very excited to see this project come to fruition and excited for what we hope will become a series of charter schools, focused on community and opportunity and the unique goals and needs of their individual neighborhoods. We want to give the power of education back to the parents, back to the community.

As you all know, most of our children's programs have always operated locally. We value our community and are proud of the work we have done. Yet, from the mouths of babes come hard truths and even harder questions.

I'd like to talk about Clarissa Collins, New York States' Teacher of the Year and one of only five teachers nationwide to receive the Horace Mann Award for Teaching Excellence. She is a third grade teacher at Ludes Elementary. Last year she began a correspondence project in her classroom that caught like wildfire and spread quickly throughout the school. Every student now has a pen pal, or a Global Companion, as they call one another, from developing and war torn countries all over the world.

She began this project to help her third graders develop better writing skills and to help broaden their world, yet so much more has come from such a beautifully simple idea. The children are engaged and curious. They are soaking in each other's culture, learning from one another and most importantly, they have started to ask questions, hard questions that we should have been asking ourselves.

I had the great fortune of sitting in on an academic block with a group of students where kindergarten through eighth grade was represented. These children stopped me in my tracks and made me think, made me question. Children see the world through unjaded eyes; they see things as they should be. I asked them why are they writing instead of sending emails; it's quicker, right? They all looked at me like I was crazy. 'They don't have computers there,' one of the older children responded in a very matter of fact tone of voice that I'm sure his mother would have appreciated. But he was right; I should know that, I do know that. And then just as wisdom comes from the most unlikely places a little first grade girl touched me on the hand and quietly asked, 'Why don't they have what we have?' As simple as that, why?

Since that day, our team has worked tirelessly to make connections, secure funding and cooperation and to make a plan of action. There is no reason why those children should not have what our children have and it is our goal to rectify this simple injustice, to give every child the opportunity to thrive and be a part of the global community.

Our first goal will be to implement improvements to the schools so they are technologically ready. We will start with the two schools that Clarissa began with and we will expand by two new schools each year. We are hugely proud of this program; the children have remained engaged and are actively involved in the planning.

As most of you know, our educational foundation has been chaired by the lovely Nadja Vladova, who lends not only her star power to our causes but her open heart as well. Nadja and I were very young when we began our first foundation. Born of new experiences and travel, we knew that with our privilege came great responsibility and together we could make a big difference.

It is with great pride and sadness that we announce tonight the end of one chapter, but the beginning of another with these two projects. Our global project will need a knowledgeable chair, and seeing as our first two schools are in the Ukraine, the amazing Nadja has volunteered to lend her expertise."

I look down and see her shift in her chair, looking around the room in surprise just as everyone looks at her. The shock on her face is priceless, but it's her keen sense that all eyes are on her that keeps her from reacting.

"Nadja will be joining our team in the Ukraine next month, her excitement about the upcoming project is infectious and we know she will make the foundation proud. It is because of this, this wonderful, selfless act by Nadja that we are left with a vacancy on the Board of Directors for the

Education Foundation. There are big shoes to fill and with the growth we are hoping for in the coming years, it is important that the most qualified and most dedicated candidates be considered.

Once again, in her selflessness and wisdom Ms. Vladova has come through for us, she has named her successor and I for one could not be more excited. This young lady will bring a fresh perspective and a sense of duty to the position that will surely help to push the Slate Family Foundation into the next phase with enthusiasm and creativity. So as we celebrate the triumphs and continued growth of our programs, we must bid goodbye to Ms. Vladova and welcome her successor, Sophie Noelle."

The veins bulge in Nadja's swan like neck as she struggles to control her reaction, keenly aware of all the influential eyes that are fixed on her. The crowd stands and roars with applause as my father walks Sophie onto the stage. Nadja's eyes bulge in exquisite anger, the color drains from her cheeks and I just smile back and take Sophie's hand.

"Now that we have all the business out of the way for the evening, let's get down to what's really important, the dancing." The bandleader takes the cue and the horn players stand and begin to play *Moonlight Serenade.* Nadja watches my every move while she is surrounded with well-wishers.

For the first time in her life she looks to escape

the spotlight but there will be no reprieve for her. As Sophie and I step off the stage we are corralled into a picture by the event photographer. My father and I flank the photo, Sophie on my arm, the other board members and Nadja in the middle, the reluctant center of attention. He stops shooting and starts giving direction while his assistant changes lenses.

"Now let's have Mr. and Mr. Slate, please." The others walk from the picture but I don't want to let Sophie go.

"It's ok, "she whispers as a tighten my grasp. "I'll be right here." I let her go and he snaps a few dozen photos of me and my father. I watch Nadja in the shadows, scowling quietly trying to slink away.

"Don't go far Ms. Vladova. I need a shot of you and your successor." The corner of her mouth curls and twitches and I smile back at her. "Thank you gentleman. Congratulations on your success this year." He shakes my father's hand then mine. "Ms. Vladova and Ms. Noelle, if you could." He gestures to where he would like them to stand but nobody moves. Sophie looks at me and with a confidence in her eyes that makes me smile with pride.

"You make me incredibly proud," I whisper before kissing her cheek and letting her go. She beams as she takes her place, as if her smile is her armor. Nadja steps into the light and forces a practiced but broken smile as she shakes Sophie's hand.

Her hand is cold and she grasps mine too hard but I just smile, knowing this is killing her. The photographer starts to snap away and she slips into her model trance, her face practiced, and her posture impeccable. Yet under her breath she cannot help herself for trying.

"You don't deserve any of this you little tramp." Her hushed words are acidic and meant to bite but I don't care any longer. I pull her closer to me and press my cheek to hers, both of us smiling brightly for the camera. She struggles to pull her hand from mine without making a scene but I tighten my grip and keep smiling. "He will get tired of you. He will replace you and there is nothing you can do to stop it."

"Just a few more ladies!" The photographer calls. I turn and kiss Nadja on the cheek as he takes the last shots.

"Have a nice time in the Ukraine," I murmur in her ear as Rhys takes my hand and thanks the photographer, urging me towards the dance floor and away from her. She watches our every step and I watch her watching us until Rhys pulls me into the fray on the dance floor and we are swallowed by the crowd. He tips his head to the band leader and they begin to play A Kiss to Build a

Dream on.

"Do I want to know what was said?" He asks as he swings me from his arms and back into his embrace.

"Nothing important." I look up into his sparkling eyes and smile sweetly giving nothing away. He lets it fall to the wayside and we dance, his arm wrapped tightly around my waist, my eyes locked firmly on his.

Ch. 23 Epilogue

The text came just as we were walking out the door.

Sophie I think it's time! We are heading to the hospital. Matthew will call you when we are checked in, see you soon! Oh my god I'm going to have a baby!!!

She paces nervously, refusing to leave for dinner; back and forth waiting for the phone to ring.

"Sophie, I had a reservation my Love. I'm sure we can have dinner first." She looks at me exasperated and unconvinced.

"We can have dinner any night; Olivia is having a baby Rhys. I can't miss it." She stops and takes my drink from my hand. "Why hasn't he called Rhys, why?"

The frustration can't mar her beautiful face but she is beyond reproach. "I think we should just go Rhys. Maybe something happened, an emergency, a complication. I really think we should just go."

"Sophie," I stand and cross the room, folding her into my arms, trying to calm her nerves, "she said he will call and he will. I am sure everything is fine, just relax. I think we should go have dinner and wait"

"Relax?" She pushes away from me, "Rhys, don't tell me to relax. Just take me to the hospital, please. Olivia would want me there; I will be devastated if I miss something." I know she would be and I realize my plans have to take a back seat.

When we arrive at the hospital Sophie jumps into gear like I have never seen, pushing Matthew from the bedside, holding Olivia's hand as they talk about a birth plan. Sophie starts barking orders at Matthew and I and we blindly oblige, taken aback by her taking charge. I watch her handle the situation and am overwhelmed. Just when I think I can't love the woman more she shows me another side of her that makes me fall in love all over again.

Olivia's labor quickly progresses and Sophie's strength grows exponentially with every contraction. She is calm and collected as Olivia begins to slip into a heavy labor. I excuse myself and take a stroll around the maternity ward uncomfortable watching Olivia in such pain.

I finger the box in my pocket, making sure it's still safely where I put it.

After two hours of labor, shouting and tears the beautiful little Lola makes her debut and she is a sight to behold. The glee on Matthews face is infectious; he pats me on the back as I congratulate him. But it's watching Sophie hold her that cements my entire future. That is it, right in front of me, the picture I want to look at for the rest of my life. The woman I want, holding the whole world in her arms. There is no perfect moment, this *is* the moment, will not let it slip away

"Sophie." She looks up at me with such love in her eyes I feel like I could burst. Overwhelmed and desperate to know her answer now I can't hold back. "Sophie Noelle," the room grows quiet as she watches me. Matthew smiles and puts his hand on Olivia's shoulder, knowing. Olivia looks at Sophie and then to me before a realization dawns on her as well and the silence is perfect.

"Sophie Noelle," I say pulling the box from my pocket. Her eyes grow wide and she starts to shake her head back and forth, careful still not to move the baby. "You are the love of my life Sophie; you've made me a better man. I cannot imagine my life without you, I don't want to." I take a step closer to her and open the box.

"Sophie, will you do me the great honor my Love." I tip the box at her and her eyes bulge. I knew no simple rock; heavy on carats would do, not for my Sophie. The diamond is small, Asher cut, in its original setting, my grandmothers setting, with a ring of emerald dust set around it. Her eyes glisten under unshed tears and she calls out to Matthew.

"Someone come get this baby," her arms tremble but the smile on her face says the words she has yet to mutter. She hands the baby off to Michael and crosses the room in an instant, falling into my arms.

"I love you Sophie, will you marry me?" I

whisper in her ear.

"Do you know how long I have been waiting to hear you speak those words?"

"Then I should hope for an answer," I tease.

"Oh I'll give you an answer Mr. Slate; I will gladly shout it from the rooftops if you like. I love you and I want the whole world to know."

Thank you so much for taking this journey with me. For reading and reviewing and supporting any authors that light your fire. Please follow me as I have so much more to share. You can find me on Facebook, Pinterest, Instagram and Twitter and I LOVE to hear from readers! Email me at
Noellebodhaine@gmail.com

As you ponder your next read may I make a suggestion? I love to share other Indies especially those who I am such fans of and proud to call friend, Alice C. Hart is one such talent! Her book Obsession hit the ground running this year and it is hot hot hot! Please enjoy the following snippet from Obsession by Alice C. Hart and check her out!

Obsession
Alice C. Hart

Synopsis

Sitting in a local downtown coffee shop, I saw her breeze in through the doors. She was strikingly beautiful. It was like lightning struck me. I couldn't keep my eyes off her. I watched her place her order. As she was about to leave, I grabbed my coat and coffee.

I headed out behind her, following her. I followed her to what looked to be a homeless shelter. She can't be homeless and I'm positive this is a men's only shelter. She must work here. What is a beauty like her doing in a place like this? She doesn't belong here. She belongs with me.

I set a plan in motion to casually insert myself into her life. It took forever to get myself in the precise place I wanted to be with her. It was almost a go. Then something happened that would change my plans. Him...

It seems my beauty has found herself someone she really likes. No matter, I'll take care of that. Abby and I will be together one day and it will be just like in my dreams.

Please note ~ this book is not intended for readers under the age of 18. This book contains adult situations, drug use, drinking, and smoking. These characters are not perfect, nor do they try to be.

Obsession: The Stalker Series, Book 1

I've always watched. I like to watch. Watching gets me off. I love the feeling of not being seen. When you watch someone and they don't know it, you inevitably learn everything about them. I only watch women; the ones that most people don't notice on a day to day basis.

Women, like that, never suspect they are being watched. Yes, the everyday woman who is single or dating, but not in a monogamous relationship, but will fuck on occasion. And you guessed it; I will watch her fuck a guy while jerking off in my own hand in order to find the sweet release I crave.

There are the beautiful moments when I get to watch a woman break out her toys and watch her make herself come. Fuckin' beautiful moments like this keep me going. Watching the pure bliss on a woman's face when she can get herself off is something I will never be able to quit. I love watching her squirm; her quivering legs, hardening nipples, her toes curling. God, I love women's feet.

Abby is gorgeous and doesn't know it. I'm positive that our life together will be nothing but pure bliss for us both. This thought excites me and I need to jerk off at the very thought of her. One day soon, she will see how much I love her, want her, need her, and then, we will build our life together.

I've never hurt anyone before. Then, I saw Abby and all the rules changed. I don't think anything could have prepared me for the force that is Abby Osborne.

I've been watching her for quite some time now, about eight months. I saw her in a coffee shop and it was like I was struck by fucking lightning. I followed her afterwards and saw she worked at a shelter and set to motion my plan to insert myself into her life.

The thing about plans is that they don't always go accordingly.

ABBY

I came screaming into the world on April 27th, 1985, at 3:33 a.m. My mother, Bonnie, was only eighteen years old when she had me. My sperm donor, I mean, my father's name is Andrew and he was twenty-one years old, and not even close to being in a place to be a father. My father once told me that he watched me being born while he was strung out on acid. I was fourteen when I received that memo.

Thanks, dick.

"I'll never forget it, Abby," he would always say to me. Well shit, I guess fuckin' not, Pops. Then he told me that they ordered pizza and were taking bets on who would arrive first, me or the pizza. I haven't seen him since.

Yes, my mother fell for a bad boy when she was only fifteen years old herself, and was pregnant with me at seventeen. My father would bounce in and out of my life periodically and it never seemed to go well. I used to ask my mother if she was positive he was my father.

Her response was always the same, 'Unfortunately, yes.'

This in itself was not starting my life out on a super path. I will, however, always look back to my mother and know she did the best she could with what she had.

My grandmother was only thirty-eight when I was born, and told my mother that I must be part devil for being born at 3:33 a. m. - she's referencing that 666 stands for the Devil's number and that clearly I will be half a little devil. She is sixty-seven now and still believes I am, in fact, half a little devil. Bless her heart.

Thank God, Bonnie was smart enough not to name me after my father. She named me Abigail Mackenzie Osborne (not my father's Italian last name of D'Angelo) which has always made me happy because I love my name, and want zero ties with my sperm donor.

My ma raised me alone and, let's face it; I could have turned out a lot worse considering my genetics.

Three years after I was born, my mom's sister, Tina, would give birth to my cousin Dallas. Tina decided to name Dallas after her father, Frank Davidson, who would never appear in Dallas' life again. Don't be sad for her. She's perfectly fine. Dallas Davidson, twenty-six years old, blonde, brown eyed, five foot nothing, pain in the ass. She's my best friend and like a baby sister to me, and I will be the MOH (Maid of Honor) for her wedding next year.

Dallas and I, alone without the other, are enough for any one person to handle. Put the two of us together and look the fuck out. We are two crazy bitches that do and say as we please. We smoke pot, giggle like idiots, call each other colorful names and we are pretty sure the rest of our family hates us when we are together. Pffft, we are awesome and think if we had our own TV show, people would watch!

How do we know this, you ask? Dallas' fiancé, Justin, has a habit of videotaping us (not in like a weird creepy way, because that's gross!) whenever we cook together, smoke pot together, or are singing like rock stars in the car. Ok, we probably shouldn't be singing, as we do sound like cats howling in heat, but embracing your inner rock star in the car is always a good time!

We roll with some other bitches, too; Amanda and Kim, and twins Nicole and Natalie. We are a fuckin' blast, at least we think so! Good times are always had by all when we are together. These bitches are my family and I love them fiercely.

***

"You fuckin' cunt, go fuck yourself!" the angry homeless man shouts. It's like they think this gets to me. I'm practically numb to name calling at this point. Working at a men's homeless shelter for seven years will do that to you.

"I'm sorry, sir, but you will need to speak to a case worker before you will be allowed back inside."

This is a normal and acceptable response for front line workers at The Shelter. I work with addicts, men with mental illness, concurrent disorders, and a multitude of other problems. It's a hard job and I try not to bring my work home with me. Some days are harder than others. Some things linger in your mind and make you a more jaded person than you were ever meant to be.

"Are you ok, Abby?" asks Jake.

"Yeah, Jake, I'm cool. It's part of the job and I'm almost used to it by now."

Fuck me sideways. Jake Jackson has got to be the hottest man I've ever laid my eyes on. There is no shortage of hot men where I work.

What's even better is when I get to play damsel in distress and have all the boys running to make sure I'm ok. Let's just call that a perk of the job since I don't have many, and working at a shelter isn't as rewarding as one might think.

"Abby, I'd like to see you in my office, if you don't mind," Jake commands, politely.

"Sure, lemme just have a quick smoke and I'll be right up." I need a smoke right now. If I didn't smoke, I don't know how I could do this job. What the fuck do people do when they get stressed out and don't smoke, anyway? I'm almost positive Jake just wants to check in and make sure I'm ok after being verbally assaulted, again, by a homeless dude.

I walk outside for my smoke and am immediately

swarmed by men asking me for my smokes. For fuck's sakes! Why did I come out the front to smoke? Telling them all no, I walk away.

I get to the sidewalk where there are far less people around, and look up at the window. I can see Jake in his office, looking at me. I put my cigarette between my lips and light up, inhaling the smoke and filling my lungs before letting out a long waft of smoke. I'm looking right at Jake. I see him grin, shake his head, and walk away from the window.

Yeah, that's right, Hottie McHotterson, I see you watching me and I like it.

Jake Jackson is about six feet tall, with a big boned, but not overly muscular frame. He's thick and solid and has dark brown hair that's short, which makes him look gangsta bad ass. I have a weakness for bad ass guys. Who doesn't? I just need to find the right combination of hotness and bad ass without the guy being a complete dickhead. I know he's got some fucked in the head ex-wife and I know all about his baby girl, Isabelle. She's so cute, I could squish her face.

I make my way upstairs to Jake's office and see him sitting at his desk. He is lost in thought and staring at the computer screen. He doesn't notice me so I lightly knock on the door, letting him know I'm here. He looks up.

"Come in and have a seat, Abby." I sit and immediately feel my palms get sweaty. Why am I intimidated by his hotness, anyway?

"Abby, I know a woman working in a men's shelter can be difficult. But, it is imperative these men have positive female role models in their lives." Jake is staring me right in the eyes. His hazel green looking into my hazel brown and I think I've stared like a minute too long.

"Jake, I appreciate the pep talk and I know you want to make sure

I'm ok, and I am. I always am. I've been here seven

years and understand what I'm working with, but thanks so much for checking on me. It's about time I pack up my crap and head home, anyway." I get up to leave and Jake stops me.

"How about I give you a ride home tonight?" Say wha? Jake and I have had this little thing where we casually flirt with each other. Since starting here, he's never asked to drive me home. My heart is racing. I need to stay cool.

"Sure, you can drive me home. I don't live too far, anyway."

I start gathering up my stuff while the next shift comes in. Jake does his shift change with the next supervisor on duty and then gathers up his stuff, and we walk down the hall towards the parking lot. Since I don't have a car, and usually take the bus, this is a nice treat. It's past midnight and he doesn't want me taking the bus home. He's probably just being careful because he thinks I let these guys affect me.

We get to his car, which turns out to be a Jeep Wrangler – black, goddamn! Did he just open the door for me? What the fuck? Do guys even still do that? I thought it was an urban legend! Oh, Jesus Christmas, he just helped me climb in and I'll be damned if I did not feel a partial hand on my ass. Should I have stuck it out more so he got the full grab? No, don't be a whore for him, Abby!

He shuts my door and I buckle in as he walks around to the driver's side and hops in.

"Like my Jeep, Abby?"

"Hell, yeah, I like it! When did you get it?" It's like he knows my weakness for Jeeps.

"Last weekend and it's one of my new favorite toys," he says with a grin, and then smirks.

He fuckin' knows he can have me. I know it. FUCK ME! Why am I so transparent?

We pull out of the parking lot and start heading to my place located in the shady part of downtown Toronto. I don't live far and there is a bar right by my apartment.

"Should we have a drink, Abby?" Deer caught in the headlights here… Someone help me, for I am weak!

"I would like that. But this isn't the nicest bar around."

"I know, I've been here numerous times, and it's perfectly fine," Jake says.

We find a booth and at the same time a waitress quickly approaches us. Her name tag says Sami. Sami smiles brightly, batting her long lashes at Jake, asking him what he'd like. Insert eye roll here.

Jake smiles at her and her batting lashes and orders a Rye and Coke for himself and an Amaretto Sour for me. He actually knows my drink!

"How do you know what I drink, Jake?" This is the first time we've hung out one on one.

"I pay attention, Abby." Jake looks me dead in the eyes. And the fucker winks at me, which causes me to blush fifty shades of red!

"Fuck, why have you been paying attention to me, Jake?" He looks at me thoughtfully for a few minutes while I'm left in awkward silence.

"I think you know why. I've been watching you a long time now, Abby. I've known you for five years now and I pay attention to things, more than you think."

I was only twenty-two years old when I started working at The Shelter. I am now twenty-nine. Jake is in his early thirties, I think?

This night can go either one of two ways. One, I play into it and see what happens, possibly making the rest of my work life awkward, for God knows how long, or option two, leave. Leave right fuckin' now.

But, I think we both know I'm not going to because I've also had my eyes on Jake, it seems, for just as long as he's been watching me. I'm only curious as to why now?

Sami returns with our drinks, smiling sweetly at Jake while I roll my eyes, again. Fuckin' blonde haired, blue eyed, big boobed girls think all guys want them. Well, my sweet Sami, this one wants me tonight. Jake confirms it when he smiles, thanks her, and locks those sweet, hazel green eyes on mine. Sami gets the hint and saunters away.

"Cheers, Abby, to finally finding the right time." I raise my glass and clink it with his. Sipping my sour goodness, I have no idea what the fuck he means. My lips always pucker on the first sip and he laughs at me.

"What's so funny?"

"Oh, Abby, I love your first sip face." Blush overload, for fuck's sakes! I know he sees it.

"Yeah, well these fuckers are sour like nobody's business. Wanna sip?"

Jake looks at me with a smile on his face, reaches over and grabs my hand, and pulls the drink towards his mouth. Hell yeah! He sips my drink and I watch his face wince a bit and then he looks at me and smiles.

"Let me take you home now, Abby." Ummmmm, whoa! Am I ready for this? I'm so attracted to him and have been for quite some time. I want him to take me home so I down my drink.

"I'm ready, Jake." He throws some bills on the table and downs his drink. We leave the seedy bar in downtown Toronto and head to my place…..

COPYRIGHT- Obsession by Alice C. Hart

LOOK FOR OBSESSION on AMAZON

www.ingramcontent.com/pod-product-compliance
Lightning Source LLC
Chambersburg PA
CBHW070826120626
46556CB00002B/664